WAY OF THE WOLF

MAGNETIC MAGIC
BOOK 1

LINDSAY BUROKER

FOREWORD

Thank you, good reader, for picking up this all-new adventure from me. Many of you know about my love for elves and dragons, but, as I've admitted before, I grew up adoring wolves and writing reports about them in school, so it was natural that I would eventually write a story with a werewolf heroine. As a middle-aged, divorced empty-nester, Luna isn't your typical werewolf, but I hope you'll enjoy sharing her adventures!

Before you start reading, please let me thank those who are helping me with this new series. Thanks to my beta readers, Sarah Engelke and Cindy Wilkinson, and my editor, Shelley Holloway. Thank you as well to my narrator for the audiobooks, Vivienne Leheny, and to Deranged Doctor Design for the book covers. Lastly, thank you, my fantasy-loving reader, for coming along on the journey.

1

———

IF SOMETHING WEIRD WAS GOING TO HAPPEN IN MY LIFE, IT WAS guaranteed to occur when I was carrying a ninety-pound toilet across the parking lot.

It was a heavy load for a forty-five-year-old woman, even one whose werewolf blood gives her extra strength, but that didn't keep me from stopping to frown at a guy wielding a metal detector. Whistling cheerfully, he swept it back and forth through the woods along the property line of the apartment complex.

With wavy salt-and-pepper hair that fell to his jaw, a tidily cultivated three days' worth of beard stubble, and a black leather jacket, he could have walked off the front of *GQ*. Had I seen his picture on a magazine, I wouldn't have thought much of it, but in person... there was something about him that put my hackles up. Something... feral.

"You can do whatever you want on the city land," I called to him, "but once you step onto that lawn, the grounds belong to Sylvan Serenity Housing." I waved to indicate the five acres of grass, trees, and pathways that sprawled around the complex's two-hundred-plus units that were clumped in several two-story buildings.

As the property manager, it was my job to shoo away treasure-hunting trespassers, even if he hadn't crossed the line yet. After almost twenty years working for the owners, I felt obligated to watch out for their interests and also for the tenants. And maybe I was a touch territorial. I blamed the wolf blood for that, even though the monthly potions I consumed kept my lupine tendencies on the down-low.

The guy looked over at me, his brown eyes widening in surprise, probably because the person addressing him held a new one-piece toilet. "Why, my lady, I wouldn't *dream* of trespassing."

My *lady*?

His accent was vaguely British but muddled, as if he'd left home a long time ago and lived many places. My experiences with James Bond movies—all watched due to my ex-husband's preferences—and Monty Python—a reflection of *my* preferences—did not lead me to believe anyone in the UK said *my lady* anymore. Nor were Europeans wandering a greenbelt in a suburb north of Seattle common. Shoreline wasn't a tourist area, especially not this stretch, with the freeway traffic roaring past beyond the woods.

"Glad to hear it. Is that your van?" I jerked my chin toward an old Roadtrek with half the back windows blacked out—or maybe blocked. The vehicle occupied a guest-parking spot. White with blue trim, it had been modified for off-roading, with large studded tires that lifted it several inches higher than usual. On the side, blue cursive writing read: *Full Moon Fortune Hunter.*

"She's a beaut, isn't she?"

"That's not what I asked. If you're not a guest of a tenant, you can't park there."

"You're very strict for... the plumber? The maintenance woman? What did you say your name is?"

"I didn't."

"Well, as a gentleman, even though we haven't had formal introductions, I feel compelled to ask if you need assistance in toting that large, ah, are you carrying a... loo, my lady?"

"A Kohler Highland with elongated bowl and quiet-close lid. Only the best for our tenants." Only the best that had been on sale and was a model that had proven reliable in the complex. Since I was the handywoman as well as the property manager, that latter was important.

"So it *is* a loo."

"You're swift."

"Actually, I'm Duncan. Duncan Calderwood. Now that you know me, who might you be?"

"The person who watches over this place." My instincts told me not to give him my name—or anything about myself. If that van was still here tonight, I would call to have it towed.

"Like a security guard?"

"I can be." I gave him my best warning glower, one that people tended to find intimidating, even if I was only five-foot-three and one-hundred and ten pounds. Not only did I have sharp canines, but enough magic lingered about me that they could sometimes sense the danger in my past, even if it had been decades since I'd been anything but a mother, wife, and employee. "By choice," I murmured to myself.

"Ah." He—Duncan—smiled, not intimidated in the least. "That burden can't be light. I believe your muscles are aquiver. Do you need assistance?"

"They're not quivering, and I don't want help." Grudgingly, I made myself add, "Thanks," though the guy rubbed me the wrong way.

He twanged even my dulled senses. If not for the potion, I might have more easily detected what was off about him. I might have *smelled* what was off.

I shook my head. The toilet was getting heavy, so the mystery would have to wait until later. I continued up the meandering walkway to A-37 while Duncan went back to whistling cheerfully and sweeping the metal detector from fern to clump of mushrooms to cedar log. What he expected to find out there, I couldn't guess. Now and then, homeless people camped in the woods, but they weren't known for stashing strongboxes full of gold and jewelry around their tents.

As I set the toilet down and fished in my pocket for the master key for the apartments, a faint beeping drifted across the lawn. From the metal detector?

Duncan bent to investigate a fern as a pair of motorcycles roared into the parking lot. The noise startled him, and he spun, raising the metal detector in both hands like a staff while dropping into a practiced fighting crouch. With those reflexes, he had to have been in more than a few skirmishes in his day.

The male motorcycle riders, neither wearing a helmet, tore through the parking lot, circling it twice as they eyed the cars. They glanced toward me, then at one of the tenants driving in, and roared back out.

I glared at them, suspicious since crime had increased in the area lately, and glanced toward the cameras mounted around the grounds. The two men had looked like they'd been scouting the place. Hopefully, the modest vehicles of the tenants hadn't interested them that much.

Duncan lowered the metal detector, waved at me, and went back to investigating the fern.

"Yeah, you're sus too," I muttered, borrowing one of the words my younger son favored.

Thinking of my boys sent a twinge of loneliness through me. Cameron had been gone for two years, but Austin had left for Air Force training only that summer. I'd only been an empty nester for a few months.

Wanting to keep an eye on my visitor, I made more trips back to my beat-up pickup than necessary to collect my tools, a wax ring, and the new toilet innards. Apparently done with the fern investigation, Duncan had returned to wielding the metal detector over the damp fallen leaves and brown needles under the trees.

A stray black cat that lived on the grounds, despite my *many* attempts to evict it, avoided me as it sashayed through, on its way to mooch from people who left food out for it. The reaction was typical. Human males still hit on me now and then, admiring my curves, olive skin, blue eyes, and thick hair that I ensured stayed black. Animals were another matter. Felines, in particular, sensed the lupine in me and either avoided me, hissed at me, or, if they could manage it, bit me.

The cat spotted Duncan in the woods and halted abruptly, its back arching and its fur going up. A hiss of pure loathing escaped its feline lips.

"Now isn't that interesting?" I murmured.

The word *feral* came to mind again. But maybe the term I wanted was *lupine*.

Could *Duncan* be a werewolf? One who, like most, didn't take alchemical substances to tamp down the need to shift into wolf form every full moon?

The cat's reaction certainly suggested *something* odd about him. That was a more extreme reaction than the stray gave to me.

If Duncan *was* a werewolf, what could have brought him here?

As far as I knew, the Snohomish Savagers—my family's pack— were the only werewolves in the area. And they didn't take well to trespassers. None of *them* consumed potions to dampen their magic, so they were even more territorial than I.

I looked at the metal detector with more consideration than before. Was Duncan looking for something specific rather than random lost prizes?

He either didn't notice the cat or ignored it. He turned his back toward the apartments—and the feline—and ambled deeper into the woods.

After staring at him for a few more seconds, the stray slowly backed away. Finally, fur still up and tail straight out, the cat ran into the parking lot to hide under a car.

"I'm only the property manager," I told myself. "It's not my job to confront lupine strangers."

Duncan shouldn't have been able to hear from that distance, but before I stepped into the apartment, he sent a long look over his shoulder in my direction. His eyes narrowed thoughtfully.

I sighed. Something told me this guy was going to be a problem.

2

TWENTY MINUTES LATER, WITH THE WATER TURNED OFF IN A-37 AND the old toilet removed, someone knocked at the door. The tenant was at work, so I answered it warily, a premonition suggesting trouble was seeking me.

I expected Duncan, coming to do more than call me *my lady*. Instead, a college-aged kid of mixed heritage stood on the concrete-aggregate patio. With a slight build, neatly combed red hair, almond-shaped eyes, and tan skin, he wore a business suit and carried an expensive man purse. Okay, maybe it was a *messenger bag*, but the gilded leather sported a Stefano Ricci logo. *Man purse* was the term that came to mind.

Past his shoulder, parked in one of the staff spots next to my dinged and dented truck, rested a gleaming blue Mercedes G-Wagon. All kinds of unlikely vehicles had entered the premises today.

"Are you... lost?" I asked the kid.

Lost and looking to be mugged? This part of Shoreline wasn't even vaguely ritzy, and I thought of the earlier motorcycle riders who'd cruised through, not to mention the metal-detecting werewolf.

Admittedly, whatever Duncan was up to, petty crime probably wasn't it. He had disappeared, prompting me to get my hopes up that I wouldn't need to deal further with him, but his camper van remained in the parking lot. Also, a faint beeping drifted out of the woods.

"No." The kid smiled at me, but it appeared forced, and he looked me up and down like I was a panhandler about to beg for change.

The jeans and flannel shirt I wore, the sleeves rolled up to my elbows, weren't exactly business-casual, the suggested dress code for the property manager, but I was in handywoman mode today, so it seemed justifiable. Besides, it wasn't as if the owners came by to check up on me that often.

"Are you Luna Valens?" the kid asked.

"Yeah."

"I'm Bolin Sylvan. My parents sent me."

Er, maybe I *was* getting checked up on.

"Sylvan, as in the owners of Sylvan Serenity Housing?" I waved to the apartment complex.

I'd met Rory and Kashvi Sylvan, but they traveled a lot, and I usually interacted with their businessperson, Ed Kuznetsov.

"Yes, I'm their son. I'm here for..." Bolin took a deep breath, one that involved baring his teeth and visibly bracing himself. "I'm to be your intern."

"My what?" I'd heard him, but my brain didn't want to process the words.

Movement in the woods drew my eye. Duncan had reappeared, and he was peering at us from behind a few ferns. No, he was peering toward *Bolin*.

Was he eyeing the expensive man purse? Hell, maybe Duncan

was interested in petty crime. If he stepped onto the lawn, I might have to tackle him. Maybe the stray cat would help me take him down.

"I'm going to be your *intern*," Bolin said slowly, probably thinking *I* was slow.

Not usually, but I didn't want to be trailed around by a college kid driving a car worth three times my annual salary. Before taxes.

Worse, what if the owners wanted to eventually swap me out with him? What if, after more than twenty years of working and living here, I was being asked to train my replacement?

"Only temporarily. Probably only for two or three months. *Hopefully.*" Bolin winced as he looked at my clothes again and then around at the apartment complex, as if it was a sleazy slum.

It was far from that. Sure, it had been built in the seventies, so it lacked modern amenities, but, thanks to me, the buildings and the grounds were impeccably maintained. The facade and interiors might be dated, but they were otherwise in good condition, and the tenants all had excellent credit histories, were gainfully employed, and paid their rent faithfully. I made sure of that.

There was nothing *slummy* about the place, and I caught myself baring my own teeth. It startled Bolin, and he stepped back.

I forced my lips to chill out, reminding myself that my canine teeth were imposing. That was something the monthly potion couldn't change.

"I'm sure it's a good job, and that you're very capable," Bolin hurried to say, not so dense that he didn't realize he'd offended me. "It's just not what I was planning on after college, not what I'd been promised. My parents always said— Well, I majored in accounting, you see. For *them*. I mean, I like numbers, and I'm decent at math, so it was okay, but when they said I'd have a job in the family business, I assumed that I would do their books and get to travel to all the places where they have investments. Like Malta and Saint Lucia and Singapore. I didn't think I'd be hounding people for rent checks at the first property they ever bought in—" Bolin's lip curled so much that his gums were visible, "—*Shoreline*."

He said it like the suburb was the sweaty unshaven armpit of the Seattle area. It was not. Sure, it wasn't as romantic or exotic as Singapore or Saint Lucia, but lots of good people lived and worked here.

"A lot of the tenants have direct withdrawals for rent, so the books aren't that hard to keep. And I track the expenses faithfully. As for duties perfect for an intern, I'm installing a toilet today if you want to help." My eyes probably gleamed with pleasure as I extended my arm into the apartment.

Bolin reeled back, as if I'd suggested he descend into a sewer tunnel to fix an effluent leak.

"I... I can show you my résumé." He looked faint.

Maybe plumbing wasn't listed as one of his core competencies. "Okay."

When Bolin opened his bag to retrieve his résumé from a leather portfolio, I glimpsed a vial of glowing green liquid and blinked. That wasn't a bottle of cologne. And was that a silver *twig* nestled in the bag next to the vial?

Bolin noticed me peering in and snapped the man purse shut.

"Are you visiting a coven for a ritual later?" I asked, curious but not that fazed.

An old witch who lived in the complex was my potion supplier, so I had passing familiarity with the paranormal in the Seattle area. After all, I'd been born into a pack of werewolves.

Beeps came from the woods before Bolin could answer. They had an odd twang to them, more like SONAR equipment than the noises the metal detector had made.

Still half-hidden behind the ferns, Duncan gripped another

device in his hands. When he noticed me looking over, he covered it and backed out of view. The strange beeping stopped.

I was going to have to confront the guy; I could tell.

"Here." Wary, Bolin handed me the paper. He hadn't answered my question about coven visitations, but he also hadn't looked puzzled by it.

I skimmed over the résumé. It listed numerous college accolades and extracurricular activities. There was no mention of *work* experience, not even hinting of a summer spent flipping burgers at *Wendy's*.

"This is going to be fun for both of us, isn't it?" I asked.

"Two to three months," Bolin said sturdily, managing not to sneer or bare his teeth again. "That's what my parents said. I need to get on-the-ground experience and prove that I'm a competent employee, and then they'll give me a *real* job in the family business. I'll have a nice office, an opportunity to travel, paid vacation time, a retirement match, and annual bonuses."

I thought about mentioning that *I* didn't get any of those things, unless bonuses included the Christmas fruitcake and gift card, but I was fairly certain Ed was behind distributing those to the property managers.

Bolin squared his shoulders. "I'm prepared to prove myself."

"Well, the toilet is this way." I extended my hand into the apartment again, though I couldn't imagine asking the kid to do more than hold my wrench. The next two to three months were going to be a huge pain in the ass. I could tell already.

Bolin didn't move from the walkway. "Don't you have any data that needs crunching? Or work orders written up or something? I like writing."

"Oh, I'm sure you're quite the wordsmith." I pointed at a line on the résumé, right under a promise of fifteen years' experience playing the violin. "Second place in the Regional Scripps Spelling Bee."

"It would have been first, but Latin and I don't get along as well as we should. Your name is Latin, you know. Luna for moon is obvious, but were you aware that Valens is Latin too? It means strength." Bolin eyed my bare forearms.

"Yeah, my pack—my *family* is originally from Italy, a long time ago."

Bolin squinted at me, and I wondered if he knew I was a were-wolf. Ed had some suspicions about that, and I hadn't been willing to lie completely when he'd brought it up. I had, however, assured him I didn't turn into a wolf when the moon was full and wouldn't eat the tenants. He'd grunted and said as long as I got the work done during the days, he didn't care what I did at night. I'd been somewhat bemused that he thought my job ended at five p.m. but had been grateful he'd been reasonable and hadn't mentioned how often tenants needed help after dark.

"You don't *really* fix the toilets, do you?" was what Bolin asked. "You call a plumber for that, right?"

"Unless things are a real mess, I do most of the repairs around the place myself. I save the business a lot of money because I've learned to—"

The roar of motorcycles sounded in the street, more than two this time. The riders who'd cruised through earlier had returned —with backup.

Six men on Harleys roared into the parking lot, five carrying baseball bats or crowbars. One gripped a handgun.

Shit. I wasn't bad in a fight, but I didn't want to launch into a battle against a biker gang with firearms.

"Call the police, intern." I waved Bolin toward the leasing office, then jogged for the parking lot, hoping that pointing out the security cameras would dissuade the intruders from starting trouble.

I hoped that, but I doubted it would prove true. As I approached, I stayed behind cover, darting from tree to bush to lamppost, not trusting that these guys wouldn't shoot me. Even if I'd only seen one gun, the rest of them could have concealed firearms.

The riders shouted gleefully in a foreign language as they roared through the parking lot. They slammed their baseball bats and crowbars into the sides and backs of vehicles, leaving dents and broken glass.

I glimpsed red-rimmed eyes in their surly faces and figured they were on drugs.

"The police are coming!" I yelled at a thug swinging a baseball bat at a parked Toyota.

Glass shattered, and the guy rode toward another target without glancing at me.

Fury surged up within me, making me wish I could still change into a wolf. Then I could have leaped on them without fear and ripped their throats out. And if they'd shot me in that form, I would have recovered rapidly from the wounds, my magical power healing me.

But after more than twenty-five years, I doubted I would ever be able to change again. I had only my humanity to rely on.

Or so I thought. A startling tingle coursed through my veins, the hot tingle of werewolf magic. Alarm rather than relief swept through me. There was a reason I'd started taking those potions. Fantasies of dealing with bad guys aside, the last thing I wanted was to turn into a wolf in the middle of the day in the apartment complex where I worked.

The hot tingle meant it was closer to time for another dose than I'd realized. I took a deep slow breath, trying to calm my body, but it was hard with motorcycle riders creating anarchy in my parking lot.

"Nobody here has valuables, you dumbasses," I yelled as one rode past, his crowbar waving in the air. "Get the hell out of here!"

"You've an interesting negotiation style," a calm voice said from behind, startling me.

Duncan.

"I'm not negotiating. I'm cussing those bastards out."

"Allow me."

Duncan stepped out into the parking lot to intercept two riders heading toward Bolin's G-Wagon with their weapons raised and savage glee in their eyes. If Duncan was armed with anything more than that metal detector, I couldn't tell.

"Idiot." I grabbed a head-sized rock from a garden bed and hurled it as one of the riders roared close.

He was looking at Duncan and didn't see my impromptu projectile coming. My blood might be dulled by the potions, but there was nothing wrong with my aim. The rock slammed into the guy's face hard enough to knock him off his motorcycle.

Duncan, wielding his metal detector like the staff I'd considered earlier, struck another rider on the side of the head. That man also fell, his motorcycle hitting the ground, the wheels still spinning.

"That's what you assholes get for not wearing helmets!" I grabbed another rock.

The guy with the gun had stayed in the back row of the parking lot, but when he saw my attacks, he rose up on the footrests. He leveled his firearm at me over the roofs of the parked cars.

I swore again and dove behind a stout cedar.

Before the man could fire, Duncan sprang onto the roof of a car as if he'd launched out of a cannon. As soon as his feet touched down, he leaped again. He flew toward the rider, kicking at the guy's face before the vandal could turn the gun on him. They both went down, Duncan a blur of movement as he managed to keep from getting tangled up with man and motorcycle.

Still gripping his metal detector, he sprinted after two more thugs roaring around the parking lot on their Harleys. They'd stopped breaking windows, and they focused on Duncan, pointing their bats at him like jousters riding toward a target.

Since the shooter was down, I leaned out from behind the tree to grab another rock. Intending to throw it at the would-be jousters, I took aim, but another rider tore toward the G-Wagon with a crowbar.

A shriek of, "*No!*" came from the walkway.

Bolin ran toward the SUV, his man purse flopped open, and the glowing green vial in his hand. He threw it at the pavement between the G-wagon and the approaching motorcyclist. Glass shattered, and visible vapor flowed out so quickly, it was as if it was alive. There was no breeze, but hazy green tendrils formed and wafted toward the man.

Nostrils twitching, he jerked his head back. His motorcycle wobbled as he clawed wildly at his eyes.

Since he was distracted, I hurled my rock at him. It smashed into the side of his head. As with my other targets, the blow was enough to knock him off his motorcycle. Without a rider, it pitched sideways, stopping shy of crashing into the G-Wagon.

Reminded of the threat to Duncan, I grabbed another rock. But he didn't need help. Not only were the two attackers he'd faced down, bleeding and groaning on the pavement, but their big motorcycles were on their sides, the engines stopped, the frames warped, and the handlebars and other parts torn off.

I stared. How the hell had that happened?

It looked like they'd been run over by a train or had crashed into a cement wall at top speed. Neither could have happened in the parking lot. There was only... Duncan.

He stood calmly in the middle of the motorcycle carnage, straightening his jacket and tucking in his shirt. Once the state of his attire again suited him, he bent and picked up his metal detector. It didn't appear damaged in the least. *He* didn't appear damaged either.

Duncan smiled easily when our gazes met, as if nothing unusual had happened, as if raw power didn't emanate from him, as if he hadn't ripped motorcycles apart with his bare hands.

"This day is getting more and more concerning," I muttered.

3

"YOU SAVED MY *MERCEDES*." BOLIN RAN UP, HIS PHONE CLUTCHED IN one hand and the man purse in the other. That vial had come out of it, but it was once again sealed.

"Yeah," I said, "your car *was* my priority."

"It's worth more than the rest of the beaters in this lot combined. I shouldn't have driven it here. My insurance agent would have dinged me for coming into such a bad neighborhood."

I bristled, wanting to defend the neighborhood as perfectly fine, but some aspects of it *had* gone downhill of late. Prior to the last few years, I had never seen a motorcycle gang around here. Or *any* kind of gang.

Duncan ambled up, pushing his wavy hair back from his face with one hand and gripping the metal detector with the other.

"That's how we negotiate where I'm from," he said.

"Where I'm from too," I admitted.

The pack didn't have much use for diplomacy. Werewolves weren't what they'd been in past generations, before the magic had faded, but they still used muscle and fang to get what they wanted.

"About what I figured." Duncan nodded knowingly at me—*too* knowingly. "Now that we've battled foul enemies together, maybe you can give me your name."

Battled foul enemies? Who said things like that?

"Where are you *from*?" I asked, and not only to deflect his suggestion.

"Here and there." Duncan waved vaguely. "I spent some years in the countryside outside of London."

"And they talk like that there?"

"I can't remember. I've been gone a long time, and it was rural enough that I didn't interact with that many people. In my childhood, I was influenced by an abundance of medieval literature, with a smattering of the fantastical when I could sneak it in."

"The fantastical? Like what? Harry Potter?"

"Those books came out after my childhood, and I prefer slightly more adult and manly fare anyway. I *adore* what's now called the grimdark genre, though I've also immersed myself in many of the original fairy tales. They were quite dark, you know. And then there are the classical tales of pirates and swashbuckling adventure. I've copies of Dumas in my van. One's a leather-bound that's more than two-hundred years old. Do you want to see it?"

"So that *is* your Roadtrek." I'd assumed so but hadn't known for certain.

"I'll confirm that with a yea or nay if you'll give me your name, my lady."

"This is Luna Valens," Bolin offered before I could tell Duncan to quit asking.

I sighed, now doubly sure I didn't want an intern.

"A most beautiful name." Duncan held the metal detector out to the side like a sword and bowed deeply.

When he straightened, I noticed an old scar above one of his eyebrows. A circular burn mark. Like might have been done with a cigarette? It wasn't noticeable from a distance and didn't detract from his looks, but I wondered how he'd gotten it.

Sirens grew audible in the distance, and I didn't ask. One of the riders didn't stir but the others hurried toward their motorcycles, either getting them upright and running again or abandoning them. A couple of the men ran toward the woods that Duncan had been exploring earlier.

I eyed him, wondering if the appearance of the police would make him scurry off. If he was a criminal, it should.

"Luna is the perfect name for one who enjoys the moon's influence," he remarked, holding my gaze.

Hell. He *did* know I was a werewolf.

It didn't surprise me, since I was fairly certain he was one, and if I could recognize my own kind, he could too, especially since *he* presumably wasn't taking an alchemical concoction to dull one's magic—and magical senses. The lack of surprise didn't keep me from wincing. I didn't trust this guy, whether he'd helped us or not. I was positive nothing good would come from him learning about me.

"My mom picked it," was all I said. "I didn't have any choice."

My surname was another matter. For the twenty years I'd been married, I had been Luna Schneider. I'd never much liked that name and had been eager to take mine back after my slimy ex had sailed off to enjoy life with his various girlfriends around the world.

"What's her name?" Duncan asked.

"None of your business." I shot Bolin a quelling look, though there wasn't any way he could know my mother's name. Even Ed didn't know about my family.

"Indeed not," Duncan said agreeably, then looked curiously at Bolin. "You've magic about you."

Bolin blinked in surprise, though it had to be surprise that someone had noticed rather than confusion about the statement.

I'd *seen* him throw that vial of whatever it had been. Nothing mundane.

"I thought it was only contained in your bag at first," Duncan continued, "but it's in your blood too."

He didn't step closer to Bolin, but he raised his nose in the air, nostrils flaring as if he were a hound testing someone's scent.

No, not a hound. A *wolf*. And that was exactly what he was doing. Once, I'd also had keen senses that could pick out odors normal humans couldn't, and I recognized the nose waving.

"Not a witch..." Duncan mused thoughtfully.

"I'm just the intern." Bolin stepped back, glancing at me.

Now that Duncan had pointed it out, I could get a gist of something paranormal about Bolin too. Usually, I couldn't tell a witch from a necromancer from a mundane donut maker, but if I was due for another dose of my potion, it wasn't surprising that I was sensing more than usual. Further, there had been a lot of strength behind my rock throws.

"You must study... Ah, yes. Of course." Duncan snapped his fingers. "You come from a family of druids."

Bolin opened his mouth but didn't speak, only shaking his head in denial.

"I came across your kind often in the Old World. They're much rarer here, though I suppose if druids would be found anywhere, it would be in these wooded wetlands." Duncan waved toward the cloudy sky, though there hadn't been any rain in two days.

A single police vehicle rolled into the parking lot, the driver sipping from a coffee mug as he maneuvered around broken glass and pieces that had flown off the damaged motorcycles. There was only one other officer in the car with him.

"I'm glad we handled the biker gang on our own," I said, feeling the pair might have been outmatched.

"Indeed. Since I've misplaced my papers, I believe I'll take my leave." Duncan eyed one of the apartment security cameras mounted on a lamppost.

I made a note to download the footage later. Duncan hadn't turned into a wolf—I wouldn't have missed noticing *that*—but it was hard for me to imagine even someone with supernatural strength ripping apart motorcycles. One of the original were-wolves of old might have—those great beasts had been tremendously powerful as they'd stalked about on two legs with thick muscles flexing underneath their short fur—but our kind had never been that much stronger than typical while in human form.

"Thanks for helping," I called after Duncan, trying not to sound grudging. Even if I didn't trust him and suspected he was up to no good, he *had* assisted us. Throwing rocks—and vials—alone wouldn't have driven off six drugged-up bikers.

Duncan lifted a hand in acknowledgment as he walked away. Instead of heading for his van, he veered toward the woods again. Still looking for lockboxes of gold under the ferns?

"He's magical," Bolin whispered, watching Duncan disappear as the police car parked.

"Apparently, you are too." I raised frank eyebrows.

Encountering people with magic in their blood wasn't that uncommon, though mundane humans couldn't usually tell unless they saw someone do something obvious, but I hadn't had an inkling the Sylvans had paranormal blood. It was possible, however, that my brief meetings with them had occurred during times when I'd recently dosed myself with my potion, when its sublimating effects were strongest. I couldn't remember.

"I'm just the intern." Bolin's smile was nervous.

I looked at the man purse.

"Thanks for helping with my car," he said, then headed over to address the police.

"You're welcome."

I debated if it would be cowardly to let Bolin handle their

questions. He was just a kid, but he *had* been the one to call them, and his family owned the complex. Dealing with the authorities always made me nervous, as their response to unearthing paranormal beings was usually to shoot first and ask questions... never.

"Luna?" came an uncertain call from a doorway.

Numerous doors and windows were open, the heads of tenants sticking warily out. It was the middle of a weekday, but so many people worked from home that one couldn't count on the place being empty.

I sighed, realizing I would *have* to let Bolin handle the police. I needed to attend to the residents and take photos of the vandalized cars for insurance claims. I looked wistfully toward where Duncan had disappeared into the woods, envious of someone with no apparent responsibilities who could treasure hunt in the middle of the day.

My phone rang. I pulled it from my pocket, expecting it to be a tenant with a problem, though most of them only had my work number. The contact that popped up made me stop and stare. Augustus. One of my cousins. One of the pack.

It had been so long since any of them had called me that it surprised me that the number was in my phone contacts. Augustus and I had been close when we'd been kids, and I'd done the werewolf equivalent of babysitting him and his brothers and sisters, but he'd turned into a surly adult, vying for leadership of the pack.

Without answering, I tucked my phone back into my pocket. Given the way the pack had spurned me for my choices, I would prefer to continue not speaking to them.

Something told me I wouldn't get what I preferred.

4

IT WAS WELL INTO THE NIGHT BY THE TIME I FINISHED ADDRESSING tenant concerns, cleaning up the parking lot, and, finally, installing the toilet, relieved that renter had returned home late so she hadn't needed her bathroom.

I always laughed at my supposed eight-to-five office hours. Since I lived in a two-bedroom bottom-floor unit in one of the buildings, it wasn't like I ever truly left work. The tenants knew where I lived, and now a weirdo werewolf with a metal detector did too.

Oh, Duncan hadn't come by the leasing office or my apartment, but his van remained in the parking lot, so he hadn't gone far. Whatever he was here for, it had to be more than searching those woods for trinkets.

Every time I walked past his van, I was tempted to call a tow truck and have it removed from the premises, but he *had* helped with the thugs. "I'll give him until tomorrow to vacate."

In the meantime, I hoped Bolin would return with a completed police report. I would need that for the insurance claims. His meeting with the authorities had taken longer than I expected, and his G-Wagon wasn't in the lot anymore. I wondered if he'd gone home to talk to his parents about the attack. Or about getting an internship at a less eventful complex.

When I returned to my apartment, I went to the medicine cabinet in my bathroom and pulled out a vial without a label. It was almost empty of the red liquid that I consumed monthly. Not a full dose.

I fished in the drawers by the sink, believing I had another full vial. But I didn't find it. A jolt of apprehension jarred me. As today's events had driven home, I needed to take the potion soon. A full dose.

My heritage had almost risen up in the parking lot. Battle always tempted the wolf to come, and it didn't help that the full moon was only a few days away.

At least, with both of my boys gone from home now, changing and losing my humanity to my wolf half might not turn disastrous. But there were plenty of other people around that I could hurt. I always worried about that. Long ago, that had happened—*more* than hurting someone had happened—and that devastating night had never stopped haunting me.

"Good thing my dealer lives in the complex." I put the almost-empty vial back into the medicine cabinet and headed for the door, trying not to beat myself up for letting my supply run low.

Life had been busy that summer with renovations to a lot of the units, along with numerous turns and placements of new tenants. In my personal life, there had been Austin's graduation and seeing him off to the Air Force.

Cameron had visited for a while too, but he hadn't stayed long. He'd curled his lip at the idea of sleeping in his old room, the one he'd shared with his brother all through school. As I'd learned, he still hadn't forgiven me for not having the money to send him to college two years earlier, so he'd mostly come to see Austin.

What was that old saying? That it was easy to love one's children but not always easy to like them?

I didn't blame Cameron that much for his attitude though. My ex had always promised the boys that there would be a college fund for them. And, for a long time, there *had* been. But Chad had emptied it before leaving the country—and abandoning me to figure out how to pay off a car loan and credit card debt on my modest income.

On the one hand, I'd always had free rent at the complex, so that was a plus. But, on the other, I didn't earn much, and the Seattle area was an expensive place to live, especially with teenage boys with enormous appetites. It had taken selling the car and two years of scrimping to scrape my way out of debt. I'd then proudly paid for my twenty-year-old pickup—an ugly hooptie, as a friend called it—with cash.

Even though I was doing better now, it was hard not to loathe my ex. He'd left without signing the divorce paperwork—fortunately, Washington didn't require that from both parties—or showing up for the legal stuff that had gone along with our parting. When he'd briefly returned a year ago, I'd lost my temper and thrown him—and all his belongings—out of the apartment and changed the locks. That had been because, among other things, I'd caught him posting photos on an account he didn't think I knew about, showing him in tropical places with drinks in hand and bikini-clad women balanced in his lap. That account and those photos had dated back to well before our divorce.

"Asshole," I grumbled as I padded along the familiar lit walkways of the complex, nodding at tenants strolling the grounds with their dogs.

Though I was happy to curse Chad's memory and hope that he had developed debilitating crotch rot, I blamed myself for not twigging to what a jerk he was sooner. For all I knew, his supposed traveling software sales job had been a farce from the beginning. I wasn't that sure where he'd gotten the money that he had contributed, however sporadically, to our household finances over the years.

I should have dug deeper into his fishy stories earlier, but I'd been reluctant to rock the boat. The boys had loved him. They probably still did.

When I reached the last apartment in a building in the back of the complex, I pulled out an envelope labeled DRUGSTORE that I'd grabbed from my purse. The monthly allotment of cash inside was for buying things like shampoo, toothpaste, hair dye, and... werewolf-sublimation potions.

Ready to pay, I knocked three times and then two times. Beatrice, a retired nurse and hobbyist alchemist with ties to the Seattle witch community, paid her rent in lump sums six months in advance and didn't care to be disturbed. But she was usually home and always answered the door for clients who knew how to knock properly.

Or so I thought. The windows were dark, and I didn't get an answer.

Where might my retired witch have gone after dark? It was hard to imagine quirky Beatrice playing bridge or pickleball at the senior center.

I knocked again, my earlier anxiety returning, the fear I'd felt in the bathroom after realizing I didn't have more doses. The night sky drew my eye, the cloud cover thin enough to make out the silvery glow of the moon through it. A moon that would be, as I'd noted earlier, full soon. If I didn't have another dose before then, would I change? For the first time in decades?

"It's not that big of a deal," I tried to tell myself.

Before I'd turned twenty, I'd changed frequently, going hunting with the pack, reveling in the chase, enjoying the flesh of a fresh kill. I'd loved being a wolf and welcomed the magic that sang in my blood.

Heat flushed me at the memories that washed over me, not only of those hunts but of how glorious it had been to be what I'd been born to be. Magical. Strong. Proud. Fearsome. It had been joyous.

Until the werewolf that I'd loved had died. Until *I'd* killed him.

My hand shook as I raised it to knock again, desperation making the thumps hard. But Beatrice wasn't home. There wasn't any point in continuing to knock.

My hand lowered to the knob, and temptation arose. I could check to see if she'd left the door open. Even if she hadn't, I had the master key for all the apartments. I could go in, find her stash of potions, and leave the cash payment, the same amount I'd been paying her these past ten years.

It wasn't breaking and entering when you were the property manager and had a key, right?

I snorted, knowing better. And yet...

I tried the knob. It wasn't locked.

As I hesitated, torn between needing that potion and not wanting to abuse the trust my tenants and employers put in me, I sensed something. Was someone watching me?

I glanced around, my eyes probing the shadows between the lamps that brightened the walkways. Nobody was in sight, neither near the building nor on the manicured grounds surrounding it, but I eyed the woods that edged the property. Might Duncan be out there? Watching me like a stalker?

No movement in the woods drew my eye, but the trees grew close together, the evergreens blocking the meager light that the cloud-hazed moon offered. In the distance, cars roared on the freeway, but their headlamps didn't penetrate the greenbelt. There could have been an army skulking in there, and I wouldn't have known, not now.

Had my senses not been dulled, I would have heard and smelled much more.

That familiar mixture of longing for the past and fear for it held me in thrall.

"The hell with it." I pushed open the door. "It's not my fault that you didn't put a personal phone number on the application, Beatrice."

Grumbling to myself, I found the light switch by the door and flipped it on. I halted before I'd gone more than a step.

The living room was empty, save for a few tufts of lint, scraps of paper, vial caps, and a pen in a corner. The bedroom carpets held the indentions where furniture had been.

"She *moved*?"

Without telling me? I would have to check, but I believed her rent had been paid through the end of the year. She should have come by to let me know she was leaving and drop off the keys. Unless...

I frowned. She was an older woman. What if she'd passed, and some family member had collected her stuff and not gotten around to turning in the keys yet?

I pushed my ponytail aside to rub the back of my neck. Since I lived in the complex, it was hard to believe I'd missed movers coming to collect everything. She'd not only had tons of furniture but all manner of jars and bottles and containers of alchemical components. The scents of some of her quirky ingredients lingered in the air: dried leaves, exotic spices, pungent concoctions, and whatever had left that odd orange stain on the wall over there...

Still, people moved in and out of the large complex every month. It was possible a U-Haul for this apartment had been here at the same time as for someone else's, and I hadn't thought anything of another van.

"I hope she's okay."

I tried not to feel selfish about immediately wondering who *else* could make my potion. Beatrice had been doing it for more than ten years, since my last alchemist had moved to New Mexico for the sun, dry air, and desert juju, or whatever she'd called it. I hadn't heard from her in years.

My senses twanged, and I spun toward the front door. I'd left it open, and I didn't *hear* anything nearby, but my instincts warned me...

Duncan leaned into view and waved. "Hullo, oh nameless overseer of this great hive of humanity."

"We call it an apartment complex, and my new... intern gave you my name." I hesitated to admit the kid held that position. Shouldn't there have been a memo?

"Yes, but you didn't invite me to use it, despite my charm and the fact that you surely appreciated my assistance with your parking-lot problem." Duncan waggled his eyebrows, then noticed the envelope I clutched and quirked his brows.

I stuck it in my pocket, never caring to explain that I had to carefully budget to keep myself out of financial trouble. "You've crossed the line onto private property again. And your van is still in the guest parking, even though you're a nomadic scavenger, not someone a tenant invited."

"The warmth of your appreciation keeps away the chill on this autumn night."

I sighed at him. "What do you want?"

Duncan looked around the empty apartment, gaze lingering on a cork in the corner of the living room.

"We don't have any vacancies," I told him, "in case that's what you're thinking."

That wasn't entirely true, as we had a couple of tenants moving out that week, but I didn't want him sticking around.

"It's not. I am quite comfortable in my mobile domicile." Duncan pointed toward the parking lot.

"You live out of your van? Imagine my surprise."

He grinned at me. "I came to see if you or any of your residents were missing keys."

"We have a lost-and-found. Did you stumble across a set of keys in the parking lot while you were tearing bits off those motor-cycles?" I eyed him, still wondering how he'd managed that, then walked outside and held out my hand.

"I found some on my excursion." Duncan nodded toward the woods, then fished numerous sets of key rings out of his pocket, most rusty, all covered with dirt.

That didn't keep him from laying them in my hands, as if certain I would want them. He deposited key ring after key ring, two padlocks, and, finally, an old bike lock reminiscent of a rope of sausage. He draped that over my arm.

"That looks like it was lost in 1973," I said.

Most of the stuff did. Whoever had dropped the keys must have long since replaced them.

"Possibly. There's not a lot of really old metallic stuff in this part of the country, though I do occasionally find some gems among the detritus." Duncan switched to an inside pocket in his leather jacket to withdraw a grimy quarter. "Look at this lovely. It was with some other coins in an old change purse I dug up. It's from 1959. Any US dimes or quarters from before 1965 are ninety percent silver."

"Does that mean it's worth a lot?"

"It's worth... something." Duncan smiled lopsidedly and placed it in my now-dirty hands with the rest of the junk. "If memory serves, there's a little under point-two troy ounces of silver in your old quarters."

"Meaning I might be able to buy a soda at McDonald's with this?"

"Maybe a soda *and* fries."

"You sure you don't want to keep it?" I asked. "It'll cost you a couple hundred to get your van out of impound after I have it towed."

His eyebrows twitched, and he glanced toward my left hand. Noting the lack of a wedding ring?

I scowled at him. "My snark is not the reason I'm divorced, if that's what you're thinking."

Duncan lifted his hands. "I didn't say anything."

"Uh-huh. Why are you lurking around here, and what do you *really* want?" I pushed the junk in my hands toward him, signaling that he could return it, and the uber valuable quarter, to his pockets.

"I've mostly achieved my goal for the day." He nodded toward the greenbelt. "It wasn't as lucrative as I'd hoped. Sometimes, the areas like that by the freeway can have all manner of valuable scrap and even personal goods that flew off into the woods after wrecks or because someone chucked something out the window during a police chase."

Why didn't I believe him?

Because he was a shifty werewolf who smiled too much. Who'd ever heard of a lupine treasure hunter?

He took back the keys and bike lock, not appearing offended by my rejection. "I'd love to tell you all about it over dinner. May I take you out somewhere?"

"No."

"Many women have found it fascinating to hear me regale them over a meal. Did I mention that I also magnet-fish?"

"No."

"I'm an expert in locating all manner of things, mundane and even magical."

I opened my mouth to deliver the third and, I hoped, final *no* but halted as a thought struck me.

If he could find magical things, might he be dialed into the paranormal world? More so than I was? Aside from taking my potions faithfully, I'd spent my entire adult life trying to pretend such things didn't exist. Trying to pass as a normal human woman. Might he know about other *alchemists* in the area?

"Where do you sell the magical items that you find?" I asked.

I doubted an alchemist would want rusty gewgaws, but if Duncan knew the paranormal equivalent of a pawn-shop owner, maybe *that* person would know where potions could be bought and sold.

"Oh, all manner of places. The underground markets, direct to a handful of dealers I know around this and other countries, and even on eBay, though the fees and hecklers make online auction sites tedious to deal with. And the *reviews*. By the heavens, if you don't properly insulate and promptly ship your imbued charms and talismans, buyers will pounce on you like WWE wrestlers springing from the ropes."

I scratched my cheek, half-wondering if I could find a potion dealer on eBay. Or might there be some reputable online alchemist I could locate on my own? Maybe, but the idea of ingesting something magical made by a stranger from halfway across the country was unappealing. It wasn't as if the FDA tested and vetted potions.

"Are you in the market for something? I know now that keys and bike locks don't interest you." Duncan smirked. "Strange lady."

"Yeah, *I'm* the strange one here."

"Exceedingly. But I'm still willing to take you to dinner. After all, I crave high-stakes adventure."

"Like dating women who think you're a toad?"

"And who repeatedly threaten to have my vehicle towed, yes. I didn't say it was a *healthy* craving."

"Few are. Do you know anyone who makes potions?" I decided to be blunt.

I didn't need to reveal what kind of potion I needed or what I would use it for. That was a secret I held dear. My kids didn't even know. Only my ex-husband did, and I would have gladly kept it from him, but he'd met me before I'd found a substance to help my... condition. He hadn't been supportive of me taking it—*he* assumed that being a werewolf was amazing and had been into me because of my lupine attributes. Maybe that should have told me long ago that he wasn't a great catch.

"*Real* potions?" I added, since there were all manner of fake witches and mystics in the greater Seattle area who cheerfully sold crap.

"Ah." Duncan tapped his chin thoughtfully and gazed around the grounds.

A fog was rolling in from the woods, and dew droplets had formed on the grass. "I've met numerous alchemists in my journeys. I've not been in this particular area long enough to have made such contacts, but perhaps I could reach out to Stanislaw in the bayous of Louisiana. Oh, or Betsy in Pitlochry. She has a huge database of contacts in the field, and she owes me a favor for finding ingredients for her. Plus, she thinks I'm a sexy beast, so she's always eager to assist me."

"I'll bet."

"Come to dinner with me, and I'll make some calls." Duncan smiled easily, but there was an intensity in his eyes that didn't match his affable manner.

Yeah, he wanted something.

"What's your favorite food? Salmon? A rare steak? Some appealingly roasted haunch of meat?"

If I'd had any doubts that he knew about my heritage, the questions would have set them aside.

"I like teriyaki. It's affordable." To some extent. I usually cooked at home, which was even *more* affordable, but I hadn't broken into my entertainment budget yet for the month. I'd been too busy to be entertained.

"Ah, a *flavored* haunch of meat. Cubed up and threaded on skewers before grilling. I would not object to such fare."

"That's good since you offered to pay." I closed the door to the empty apartment, making a mental note to dig into the records and see what contact information I had for Beatrice. I'd made sure she put *some* phone number in the field and believed she'd said it had belonged to a relative.

"Indeed I did. Allow me to escort you to my van."

"Pass." I brushed past him to lead the way to the front of the complex. There was no way I would get in that van with him. For all I knew, it was filled with iron shackles, torture devices, and guns loaded with silver bullets. "I'm not carpooling with a stranger. I'll meet you there."

"Are you sure? I'd love to show you my giant magnet."

"Save it for Betsy. I'll meet you at the teriyaki place on Bothell Way." I didn't intend to invite him into my car any more than I was willing to get into his. Besides, if he had to drive his own van, it would leave our parking lot. Hopefully permanently. "I've done a few repairs for them, so they always give me big portions."

"Excellent. I like a hearty meal. I have a feeling you do too."

Yes, unfortunately. The potion dulled many of my werewolf attributes, but I paid for being stronger than normal by having a fast metabolism.

When we reached the parking lot, I realized I didn't have my purse and keys. "I need to grab a couple of things." I waved toward my apartment. "I'll meet you at the restaurant."

"Yes, my lady." Duncan bowed before opening the door to his van.

When he slid it open, I glanced inside before leaving. I didn't *see* guns or shackles, but there was a wall of racks that held SCUBA gear and other equipment I couldn't name. The Roadtrek had definitely been modified from its original camper-van layout and duty.

"Bothell Way," he called. "That runs along Lake Washington, doesn't it?"

"Through part of Kenmore, it's close to the water, yeah."

"I've never magnet fished in Lake Washington. Are there lots of docks? It could prove fruitful."

"I don't know, man. Just don't forget to reach out to your alchemist contacts." I shook my head, afraid I was, at best, wasting my time. At worst, this guy could turn into a kidnapper or murderer and kill me.

As I unlocked the door to my apartment, a howl sounded, rising above the distant roar of freeway traffic. A wolf.

I looked back toward the van, but Duncan was driving out of the parking lot in human form. That hadn't been him.

5

When I turned into the unassuming teriyaki restaurant, the Roadtrek wasn't in the parking lot. I poked into the envelope in my purse labeled ENTERTAINMENT to make sure I had sufficient funds. Duncan had offered to pay, but I had no intention of putting out, or whatever he expected, and would make that clear by covering my own meal. Assuming he showed up.

After waiting a few more minutes, I wondered if Duncan had gotten lost or decided I wasn't worth the effort. The latter seemed unlikely since he'd been so persistent about asking me to dinner. For reasons known only to him. I was attractive enough that persistent men weren't puzzling, but such attention wasn't as frequent as it had been twenty years earlier.

Minutes passed, and the van didn't show. I watched a couple enter the front door and debated if I wanted to pay for takeout if Duncan didn't arrive. Back home, I had leftovers that I could eat.

The door opened again, and the smells of grilled chicken and beef wafted out. My stomach rumbled, answering the debate for me.

When I got out of my truck, I spotted Duncan's van. It was

parked across the street and halfway down a side road leading to the lake. And was that Duncan out on a dock by those condos? Half-shrouded by the fog creeping in from the water?

I rolled my eyes, wishing I'd asked for his number so I could text him to get his ass over here. Maybe he'd thought I would spend an hour putting on makeup. As if I was going to dress to the nines for dinner with a strange werewolf at a teriyaki joint.

During a lull in traffic, I jogged across busy Bothell Way. His back to me, Duncan heaved something on a rope out into the lake. The giant magnet he'd spoken of? Maybe that hadn't been a euphemism. Or not *only* a euphemism.

Whistling cheerfully, he reeled the rope in hand-over-hand.

I walked out on the dock, and he grinned over his shoulder at me, as if he'd known where I was all along.

"I've got a big one," he called.

That prompted me to roll my eyes again. "Is this how you're planning to pay for dinner?"

"You never know." Duncan leaned over the railing, whatever he'd caught right below him now. Something heavy made his muscles flex under his jacket as he pulled it up.

"Wouldn't it be easier to fish coins out of a fountain?"

"Oh, it's rarely coins you find, especially in this country, where none of the currency is magnetic." Duncan tugged a large metal frame covered in seaweed, rust, and slime out of the water. It was attached to a cylindrical magnet several inches thick.

"Is that a bicycle?"

"Looks like it is. Not much value there, alas. I've found lock-boxes before with jewelry and silver coins inside."

"I imagine it's exceedingly common for people to hurl their valuables into lakes."

"Well, it happens. Sometimes, there are wrecked ships full of goodies. This lake connects with Puget Sound and eventually the Pacific Ocean, doesn't it?"

"Through the ship canal, yeah, but I'm not aware of a lot of sea battles that took place in Lake Washington during the various wars."

"More than battles can wreck a ship." Duncan laid the bike frame on the dock and pulled with both hands to detach it from his magnet—that thing had a seriously strong pull. Other smaller items clung to it as well. He tugged off a fork and held it aloft, as if it were a great prize.

"That's not going to pay for dinner."

"You don't think this missing cutlery may have belonged to your restaurant? They could be eager to have it returned."

"The cutlery there is plastic."

"So it's a fine-dining establishment."

"Yup, just as my fancy tastes require."

Duncan pulled off a couple of rusty nails and tossed them into a garbage can ten feet away. He had good aim.

"Ah!" He slipped what might have been a coin into his pocket. It was so covered in grime that it was hard to tell.

"That one was metallic?"

"A Dutch guilder. Pre-euro era. They are metallic, yes. Your lake must have had a European visitor." Duncan hefted the magnet out into the lake again, the splash muffled by the fog.

"Seattle is a world-class city that attracts tourists." I was less certain about the suburb of Kenmore.

"I call this the drag-and-drop method." Duncan walked along the dock railing back toward shore, pulling the rope attached to his magnet behind him. "People drop stuff from boardwalks and piers all the time."

"Is this how you make a living?" I had no idea how much a guilder was worth, but I doubted it was more than the quarter he'd found earlier, and those were the only two things of value, at least that he'd shown me, that his day's work had gotten him.

"It is."

I eyed the slimy, rusty bike frame. "I'm beginning to see why you live in a van."

Since I'd lived in the same apartment for twenty years, I supposed I couldn't knock anyone for not aspiring to great wealth, but at least my home didn't have wheels.

Not visibly offended, Duncan offered a friendly nod as he reached the start of the dock and pulled his magnet up. "People pay me to find things sometimes too. I've a lot of experience and a knack for locating lost objects." This time, a short pole—or was that a tire iron?—and a blackened rectangle came up on the magnet. He pulled the tire iron away, tossed it to the dock, then plucked off the rectangular object. It wasn't rusted, but grime covered it. "iPhone."

"Given its pristine condition, I'm sure you can get a lot for it. Look, speaking of locating things, those contacts you mentioned who might know local alchemists..."

"I left messages on the way over. Email for my European contact since it's early in the morning over there. I'll let you know what they say, assuming you're still willing to dine with me."

"I do enjoy a good meal bribe. I'm ready as soon as you fetch enough to pay for your half."

"I—" Duncan had been about to toss his magnet out again, but he lowered it and frowned toward the street.

In the few minutes we'd been talking, the fog had grown thicker. Traffic rumbled past on Bothell Way, headlights muted but the drivers slowed little by the haze.

The howl I'd heard at the apartment complex before leaving sounded again, audible over the traffic. I closed my mouth, the hair rising on the back of my neck. I'd driven almost five miles to get here.

"Anyone you know?" Duncan slanted me a sidelong look.

"No."

At least, I didn't think so. Cousin Augustus's phone call came to mind.

In the days before I'd started taking the potion, when all of my senses had been keener, even when I'd been in my human form, I'd been able to pick out the differences in howls. It was similar to how a person could tell someone by their voice. But now... As far as I could tell, that howl could have belonged to a werewolf or a timber wolf escaped from the zoo. The fog also affected the clarity of the sound.

"Is there a pack that claims this territory?" Duncan asked.

"The Snohomish Savagers claim all of Snohomish County and a few miles into King, yes. They spend most of their time in northern Snohomish County though. There are a lot more farms and forests there, fewer urban areas."

The howl sounded again, closer now.

"I assume they patrol all the territory they claim and object to lone wolves." Duncan drew in his magnet and coiled his rope, done fishing for the night.

It hadn't occurred to me that the howler might have something to do with him rather than me. Maybe it should have. The pack had ignored me since I left. My mother had never even met her grandkids.

"I'm guessing I wouldn't be able to talk the woman who wants to have my van towed into vouching for me," Duncan added.

"You're suspicious, so, no. Besides, I'm not..." I didn't want to explain my past or the choices I'd made in my life to a stranger, so I groped for a way to finish that sentence. "My word wouldn't be sufficient to vouch for anyone, not with the pack."

"Are you an outcast?" Duncan eyed me contemplatively.

"I left by choice." I wondered if he could sense that the potion dulled the werewolf in me, making me closer to a normal human with no ability—no irresistible drive—to change. Or it usually did.

When its effects weren't wearing off. When I didn't need the next dose.

The fog thickened and curled around our legs, so dense that I could barely see my shoes. There was a taint to it, something unnatural that kept the hair on my neck raised and sent a chill through me. The cool, damp air smelled faintly of spent magic, a distinct odor that reminded me of the sizzle of lightning striking mixed with the scent of mushrooms dug straight from the night soil.

Twenty or thirty feet inland from the dock, two red almond-shaped dots appeared, like glowing eyes staring malevolently at us. I gaped. Those *were* eyes.

The fog shrouded the body of whatever they belonged to, but their height made me think of a big dog. Or... a big *wolf*? I almost thought *werewolf*, but my kind didn't have glowing eyes. Of course, neither did regular dogs or wolves. Was this some apparition? Or an illusion or projection created to scare us?

To scare *me*?

Duncan stood calmly, though he crouched, his rope and magnet in hand, as if he might use them as a weapon. The magnet was heavy enough to do damage if it clubbed someone, but it was hard to imagine being able to sling it fast enough and accurately enough to strike a wild animal.

The fog stirred, and two more sets of eyes appeared to either side of the first. Up the hill, traffic continued to pass, the drivers unaware of wild animals—wild *somethings*—nearby.

"Those aren't werewolves," Duncan said.

"Just normal glowy-eyed pups, huh?"

"They're being magically controlled."

"Are you hypothesizing that because of logic? Or can you tell with your senses?"

Two more sets of eyes appeared. The odds of us surviving if the animals attacked were looking poorer and poorer. I glanced at

Duncan's van, wondering if we could sprint to it and get inside for protection. Unfortunately, to reach it, we would have to run *through* the growing pack.

Duncan slanted another sidelong look at me. "You *can't* tell?"

I opened my mouth but didn't know what to say. The last thing I wanted was to explain that I voluntarily dulled my werewolf senses.

The lead animal snarled. That sounded lupine, not canine.

The fog stirred, and the wolf charged toward the dock. No, toward *me*. Not glancing at Duncan, its focus—its target—was unmistakable.

"Shit." I lunged and grabbed the tire iron, the heavy rod wet and slick with grime.

Duncan stepped away from me so he could twirl the heavy magnet on the rope. Claws clattered on the wooden dock as the wolf ran onto it. As I hefted the tire iron over my shoulder, Duncan sent the magnet flying. It sailed toward the wolf, straight at its glowing red eyes.

Despite its focus on me, the animal saw the attack coming and sprang to the side. But Duncan's throw had been fast and hard, and the magnet clipped the possessed wolf in the shoulder. It faltered and stumbled toward the railing.

Unfortunately, the rest of the pack was on the move now, charging up the dock toward me. A whisper of the supernatural crept up my spine again. I *could* feel the magical influence in the air, some tendril of power compelling the creatures to attack.

As they drew closer, big furry bodies emerging from the fog, I could tell they weren't all wolves. Some were large mutts, maybe stray dogs gathered from the area. That didn't keep them from snarling and slavering like rabid animals, ready to tear me apart.

Heart hammering in my chest, I braced myself with the tire iron.

Duncan roared and sprang in front of me, sounding more like

a wolf than a man. He blurred as he moved, kicking one animal in the jaw as he spun to grab another.

One wolf darted around him to reach me. I swung the tire iron, those glowing eyes promising me this creature wouldn't be deterred by anything less than a stunning blow.

The heavy rod connected with a thud, opening a gash under the wolf's ear, but the animal's momentum carried it toward me.

I sprang back, the slick metal rod almost escaping my grip, but I clenched down. Another animal made it past Duncan, so I dared not lose my only weapon. When I'd had the power to turn into a wolf, I'd *been* a weapon, but I couldn't do that anymore. Or so I assumed. As the scent of blood reached my nose, a flood of memories and magic flowed through me. Dormant instincts flared, and I could feel the wolf inside, scattered and hesitant after so long, but present.

As the new threat rushed me, I almost called to the magic, tempted by it. As a powerful wolf, I could quash these meager enemies. I could—

Duncan snarled and hurled one of the mutts over the railing, its snapping jaws nearly catching his ear as he heaved it away. It splashed into the water, and cold spray spattered my cheek, startling me. The wolf magic within me retreated.

More snapping jaws angled toward me, one of the red-eyed creatures that had made it past Duncan. It had hesitated—sensing that I might change?—but now it sprang.

I had only the tire iron with which to defend myself, but it worked. I caught the animal in the jaw, knocking its head aside. Glad I retained some of my heritage's strength and speed, I swung again. The tire iron took my attacker in the top of the skull.

The powerful blows should have felled the mongrel, but, driven by magic, it leaped at me again. I scurried back, adrenaline giving me speed. I should have escaped its sharp fangs, but my hip bumped into the railing, and one of the animal's canine teeth gouged my arm. I yelped in fury and pain and swung the tire iron again, knocking my assailant back.

Meanwhile, the pack leader that Duncan had hit returned to the fray, charging straight at me. I clubbed the closer animal again, trying to knock it into the water. The leader sprang toward me before I could turn to defend against it. Duncan whirled and lunged, catching the big wolf by the torso. As if it were a shih tzu instead of a hundred-and-fifty-pound deadly animal, he hefted it and hurled it over the railing.

With that enemy gone, I focused on the mongrel attacking me. Again swinging the tire iron, I managed to knock it off the dock. The canine landed with a splash shortly after the leader tumbled in.

Arm burning in pain, I gritted my teeth and hefted the tire iron in anticipation of another attack.

But we had—mostly *Duncan* had—cleared the dock. He spun toward me, his eyes savage, and his fingers curled, like claws ready to rake.

I tensed, recognizing the animalistic gleam in his eyes, the promise that he was close to turning into a werewolf. Even when the moon wasn't full, passion, fury, or the heat of battle could bring out the wolf. I knew all about that.

But Duncan seemed to recognize that I wasn't a threat. After a tense moment, he lowered his arms. He shook his head, his wavy hair flopping about his jaw, and tamped down the wolf within. The next time he met my eyes, he was smiling, the savageness gone.

"I knew dinner with you would be interesting." Only a hint of an animalistic rasp to his voice suggested how close he had come to changing.

If he had, would he have attacked me? Or would he have recognized me as an ally?

The pack always knew its own, but he'd implied he was a lone wolf. He might be one of those werewolves who couldn't tell friend from foe when he changed, who was overcome by savage instincts and attacked any that those instincts deemed a threat, not coming back to his rational mind until the magic wore off and he reverted back. I knew all about that too.

"We haven't even gone into the restaurant yet," I said, not voicing any of my concerns. After all, we hadn't yet admitted, either of us, to being what we both knew the other was.

"Of course not." Duncan glanced at the wolves and dogs in the water, but they were all swimming away, and no more red glowing eyes were turned in our direction. He plucked up the fork he'd found earlier. "We're still collecting the cutlery."

I couldn't manage a return smile for his stab at humor. Instead, I eyed the bleeding gash on my arm and thought of his earlier words. Reluctantly, I admitted those animals hadn't attacked us because Duncan was a lone wolf. For some reason, someone was after me.

"Do you need to see a doctor?" Duncan asked, noticing the wound. "I assume you're impervious to rabies, but..."

Yes, as far as I knew, the regenerative power of the wolf protected our kind from such maladies. Besides, that pack of strays hadn't been driven by madness but by magic.

"I'm fine. I heal quickly."

"I imagine so."

Another howl sounded in the distance, this time with an edge of irritation to it. I had heard of werewolves capable of controlling lesser dogs and wolves, but this was my first time seeing it. Of course, I hadn't spent any time around my own kind these past twenty-five years. Whoever the howler was, he sounded irked that his minions hadn't been successful.

"*That's* a werewolf." Duncan lowered the fork.

"I know."

What I didn't know was whether or not, if Duncan hadn't been with me, the werewolf would have come in person to attack me. To... *kill* me.

6

AFTER SPENDING THE MORNING GOING OVER THE BOOKS TO MAKE sure I was balancing them correctly—it's always a joy to have someone half your age checking your math—my intern brought over a list of maintenance requests that tenants had filed.

"Do you want me to make calls and arrange appointments for contractors to come out and give estimates?" Bolin asked. "Or are these the kinds of repairs you handle yourself?"

I perused the list, glad for the distraction. We were sitting in the leasing office while rain fell outside, pattering off the walkways. I'd been answering tenant emails and inquiries about vacancies, but I'd also kept glancing at my phone, wondering if I should call my cousin back.

Augustus hadn't left a message, so maybe it had been a butt-dial, and he hadn't meant to reach out. If so, it had been the first time his butt had chanced upon my number in years. Decades? As with the rest of the pack, he'd ignored me since I'd left. No, since I'd started taking the potion. Leaving and turning one's back on one's family was offensive, but leaving and turning one's back on one's heritage... That was unacceptable.

If I hadn't been so sure that Duncan wanted something from me, I would have been surprised *he* was talking to me.

The night before, as promised, he'd offered to buy me dinner, even producing normal currency—not grime-coated coins from past decades. I'd declined, insisting on paying for my meal, but I had spent an hour with him while we dined on chicken skewers, Asian slaw, and rice doused in teriyaki sauce. The fact that he'd ordered four extra skewers and barely touched the sides attested to his carnivorous ways. The wolf in me also craved meat, but I'd never made enough money to buy heaps of it, so I'd learned to make do with grains and vegetables. Besides, that was what *normal* humans ate, and I'd never wanted to stand out in a suspicious you're-clearly-a-dangerous-paranormal-predator way.

During our meal, Duncan had been an agreeable enough companion. And, when he'd gazed pensively off into the distance, I'd caught myself noticing how handsome his profile was. His usually present smile and frequent winks made him look a touch goofy, but he'd been anything but that when he'd been fighting. He'd been... amazing.

Bolin cleared his throat, and I blushed, turning my attention back to the list of maintenance requests.

"I can wash the bird poop off the outside of D-43's windows," I murmured, ignoring his lip curl. Such an activity was probably beneath a scion of the Sylvan family. Maybe I would bring him with me and make him hold my begrimed scrub brush. "And let's go take a look at this leak and see how bad it is. I usually call Alex or José if a plumbing job is going to involve cutting into the wall or ceiling. And if there's mold that needs to be remediated... that's the worst. Tenants can sue over mold."

"When you say *let's*, do you mean you want me to come with you?" Bolin looked longingly toward the desk and computer, as if the spreadsheet pulled up was more appealing than doing physical labor.

I couldn't imagine feeling that way. "Yeah, it means let *us*. Did you study contractions for your spelling bee?"

"No. I studied Latin and Greek rules regarding word origins."

"Fascinating." I grabbed my toolbox. "You can tell me about them while you hold my wrench."

"Are you really interested?" Bolin gave me a wary-hopeful look. Not sure if I'd been sarcastic and was mocking him?

One probably shouldn't quash the passions of one's intern, no matter how much one didn't *want* an intern.

"I'm not *un*interested," I offered as we headed out the door.

"Does that mean you've never been inclined to research the subject matter but also wouldn't fall asleep while I waxed poetically on orthography?"

"I almost never fall asleep while I'm in the middle of fixing leaks, so your odds are good of a semi-alert pupil."

"Oh," Bolin said brightly, trotting after me, maybe reading more enthusiasm into my comment than I'd intended. "Did you know the word *orthography* comes from the Greek root of *orthos,* which means *right* or *correct* and *graphein,* which means *to write*?"

"Fascinating."

As my intern went into more depth, I picked up the pace, following a walkway through the rain and over to the next building. I waved, almost relieved to find the twenty-something tenant waiting outside in front of his unit, the overhang protecting him from the weather. With a laptop bag slung over his shoulder, he was ready to head to work.

When he pulled out an inhaler and took a hit, my relief evaporated. Whether he meant it to be or not, I had a feeling that was a condemnation of the air quality inside his apartment.

"Hi, Mr. Davis," I said. "You heading out for the day?"

That would give me time to resolve the leak issue as much as possible before he returned.

"Yeah. In a minute." Davis nodded for us to go in.

Before stepping inside, I looked past the lawn and toward the greenbelt. After the previous night's attack, I now expected to spot red eyes glowing from the shadows under every tree. I didn't, but I'd had the feeling of being watched every time I'd walked outside that morning.

Later, I would call Augustus. As much as I dreaded his snark and condemnation, I had to figure out what was going on.

"The leak is in the ceiling." After breathing in a second puff of his medicine, Davis visibly braced himself and walked inside.

Even before we reached the bathroom, I could smell the musty scent permeating the apartment. Definitely mold. It was, as far as I was concerned, the scourge of the Pacific Northwest.

"I noticed that discolored spot a while ago." The tenant pointed toward the ceiling over his toilet. "And it's been getting larger. Now there's water dribbling down the wall."

Since I was, as my boss Ed always assured me, in the customer-service business—AKA the customer-*pleasing* business—I kept myself from asking why Davis hadn't brought the leak to my attention when he'd first noticed it.

"We'll get it handled as soon as possible," I said instead.

Davis looked curiously at Bolin.

"That's my new intern," I said. "He's great at plumbing. What's the root of the word plumbing, Bolin?"

"Ah." Bolin's expression was one of protest, but he did offer, "The Latin *plumbum*. That means lead because they had lead pipes back then. It contaminated the drinking water, and some historians believe that lead poisoning was common and contributed to gout in the Roman armies. It may have been behind the infamous madness of Emperor Caligula. It could have even led to the downfall of the entire Roman Empire."

"Poisoning?" Davis lowered his inhaler and stared up at the water-stained ceiling.

"We don't have lead pipes." I resolved not to consult Bolin on any more word origins, at least not in front of tenants. "We'll get this fixed up. Why don't you head to work, Mr. Davis?"

He nodded and hustled for the door, doubtless eager to escape the musty air—or perhaps his incipient lead poisoning. I sighed.

"I don't suppose you have a potion in there—" I waved at Bolin's fancy leather bag, nobly resisting the urge to call it a man purse, "—that fixes mold?"

We couldn't see any green fuzz growing on the ceiling, but my nose promised me it lurked behind the damp drywall.

"I don't have *potions*," Bolin whispered and glanced around, as if an eavesdropper or smart device might be listening. The latter wasn't that uncommon in the apartments anymore. I was always careful not to scratch my butt or fart too loudly on my maintenance calls.

"What'd you throw in the parking lot yesterday?" I hadn't asked him then, and had almost forgotten about it, but that concoction *had* been useful. It occurred to me that he—or maybe his globetrotting parents—might know of an alchemist who could supply me. Even if Duncan could find someone, I would prefer not to be beholden to him.

"A chemical compound not dissimilar to a smoke grenade."

"It looked like it might be an *alchemical* compound."

Bolin eyed me warily. Worried I would rat him out for having ties to the paranormal world? To, if Duncan had been correct, a druid family?

With secrets of my own, I wasn't inclined to blab about anyone else's.

"I know a thing or two about the paranormal," I offered. "I'm not bothered by people who practice the various arts."

"Oh." Bolin's wariness turned to relief and then curiosity as he looked me up and down. "When we first met, I thought... You seem a little... I'm not sure."

"I get that a lot." I smirked at him.

He didn't appear amused. "In college, I got into some... stuff. My mom doesn't know. My dad... might, but he doesn't talk about magic when she's around, and he changes the subject if *I* try to talk about it. I don't know why. My grandpa—my dad's dad—was from Ireland. I'm not supposed to know, but Dad studied magic with Grandpa before he passed. Dad can read Gaelic and has books on druid stuff in his office—he tells Mom that they're history books, but *I* know better." Bolin lowered his voice. "My grandpa was a druid, and, when I was a kid, he said I had the knack. But Mom shooed him away when he said that, and Grandpa didn't come around the house after that. Mom wanted me to grow up to be *normal*."

"Yeah? Was she the one who thought violins and spelling bees were good ideas?"

"Extracurricular activities help with college applications and scholarships. And normal people play musical instruments." Bolin scowled at me in defiance. "I do admit that the summer I tinkered with the theremin may have gotten me picked on by the neighbor kids."

"Kids are mean," I said to be sympathetic—and because I wanted to know if he had a potion supplier. "Where do you get your chemical concoctions?"

"My dad has a stash that my mom doesn't know about."

I slumped with disappointment. He didn't have a supplier, just whatever his father kept in a desk drawer. It was highly unlikely a real-estate investor and businessman—even one with druid tendencies—would have werewolf-sublimation potions in his office.

"I'm not supposed to know about his stash either," Bolin added, "but I've always been a curious sort."

"Is that a way of saying you're a huge snoop?"

"I'm barely five-foot-six and weigh in at one-twenty. I'm not a huge anything."

"So a small-to-medium snoop."

That earned me another scowl.

Bolin had probably been beaten up in school, especially if he'd regularly informed his peers about the roots of words. Maybe that was what had prompted him to get into the druid stuff. I imagined him slinging potions—chemical concoctions—at bullies.

"Well, if your dad has anything that can eradicate mold, I would pay for that." I eyed the leak and pulled out my phone to call one of the contractors we worked with.

"Druid magic usually enhances and stimulates plant growth, not the other way around."

"Mold isn't a *plant*. It's an infestation."

"It's technically a fungus, so it would be more of a colonization than an infestation. Also, it's a natural part of the environment."

"Not when it grows in walls and turns my tenants asthmatic." The call dropped to voicemail, and I left a message.

"It *might* be possible to convince it to grow elsewhere." Bolin scratched his jaw thoughtfully. "I'd have to do some research, and you'd have to remove the water source."

"That's the plan. I—" My instincts warned me of someone magical approaching.

Phone tucked back into my pocket, I stepped out the front door.

Duncan was ambling up, his affable smile on his face. That didn't keep me from remembering how he'd fought the night before or how he'd *almost* changed into a much more dangerous version of himself.

A weird sensation teased my gut. It might have been dread, foreboding, or the nervous anticipation of... something.

"I hope you don't mind," Duncan said, "but I parked in the staff spot next to that gleaming Mercedes SUV. The guest parking was full."

"You're not a guest. That parking was never for you."

"After all we've been through together, I'm not a guest?" Duncan planted his palm on his chest as he raised his eyebrows. "I'm aggrieved."

"You're *definitely* not staff." I resisted the urge to threaten to have his van towed. We *had* been through a lot in the last twenty-four hours. I didn't trust him, not in the least, but it was hard to deny that he'd helped me out. Twice.

"That's my car." Bolin leaned out of the apartment to look at us.

Duncan eyed him, all twenty-two years of him. "You buy Bitcoin when it was cheap or something?"

"No, my parents bought rental properties when they were cheap." Bolin waved at the complex.

"Ah, so you're privileged and spoiled?"

"I..." Bolin glanced at me, as if I might prove his defender. "I admit to enjoying privilege. Thanks for keeping those bikers from vandalizing my car yesterday."

"I do try to help people." Duncan bowed to him, then focused on me. "Might we talk privately, my lady?"

"You're not going to ask me on another date, are you?"

"That's not why I came, no, but I did find last night quite stimulating and invigorating."

Bolin made a face and squeezed past Duncan, hurrying toward the leasing office.

"I'll go start that research," he called back.

"Research?" Duncan asked curiously.

"We have a mold colonization."

Duncan sniffed toward the doorway. "Ah. Quite."

"Thanks again for your help yesterday," I made myself say, though my mistrust for him made the words come out grudgingly, "but what do you want? I'm not looking to stimulate or invigorate you again." Once more, I glanced toward the woods, hoping that would prove true.

"You asked about potion suppliers."

I grew less grudging and more hopeful. "Yes, I did."

"One of my contacts got back to me about a promising local person. She doesn't know the alchemist's phone number, but she did share an address, so we can go visit. Or you can if you don't want to spend more time with me. I'll allow that's a possibility, however puzzling I find it."

"I haven't figured out why *you* want to spend time with *me*." I looked frankly at him.

Without hesitation, he said, "Because of your conveniently placed parking lot adjacent to those enticing woodlands."

"Uh-huh. I'm sure the greenbelt next to the freeway is a treasure trove waiting to be pillaged."

"It's not without merit. And the view isn't bad either." He smiled, then gave me a deeper bow.

"I turn forty-six this winter, I'm not wearing any makeup, and nothing in my wardrobe is sexy." I plucked at the men's Henley that I usually threw on anytime I expected to end up under sinks or in crawlspaces. "I'm not sure I even rubbed on my wrinkle cream this morning."

Okay, I didn't have any legitimate *wrinkles* yet, but the creases in my forehead had grown more noticeable of late. For the first time in my life, I was contemplating bangs. I'd *already* had to dye my hair, thanks to the insidious grays that had appeared at my hairline.

"And yet your radiant beauty is like that of the sun, a sizzlingly appealing beacon that must continue to draw men of all ages."

"Say more crap like that, and I'll renew my threats to have you towed."

"You're a hard woman to woo."

"Because I don't *want* to be wooed. The last time I let that happen, I ended up with two kids. Two kids who are now *adults*, I'll point out."

Technically, Austin was only eighteen and had the maturity of a labradoodle, but I trusted the Air Force would turn him adultish before long. If nothing else, he would have to learn to do his own laundry.

"Growing old is to be cherished. Not everyone gets to do it. I recently turned fifty and am often befuddled that I've managed to live long enough to gain silver streaks in my pelt." He pushed a hand through his salt-and-pepper locks.

"Silver? You're not a precious metal. Those are patches of gray."

Unflappable, Duncan lowered his hand. "Despite your prickly demeanor, I will relay the message my contact gave me. She suggests bringing any remains you have of your existing magical concoction, including a list of ingredients, if you know them. I wasn't entirely sure what your potion is but thought I might have the gist and mentioned it to her."

I struggled between wanting to bare my teeth—I didn't want anyone *gisting* about my private potion use—and being appreciative that he had a lead for me.

"My contact wasn't familiar with a potion that does what I think yours does and said the local alchemist might need to do some research," Duncan continued. "The more information you can give her, the better. Do you know what it's made from?"

"Sort of."

"Hm."

"I can find out." How, I didn't know, since only a few of the ingredients were written on the labels, but I would attempt some research. "Thanks."

I lifted my hand, intending to shoo him toward the greenbelt, but hesitated. Duncan kept *helping* me. Even though I mistrusted him, I did appreciate that. And if I kept snarking at him, it would be bitchy. I was probably *already* being bitchy.

With a sigh, and the fear that I would regret it, I asked, "Would you like a cup of coffee before you return to... *work*?"

I waved toward the trees, not fully able to take the sarcasm out of the word. If he made enough money to live on by scavenging in the woods—and the lakes—I would be shocked.

Duncan beamed a smile at me. "I would *love* a cup of coffee."

That smile appeared triumphant, and my certainty that I would regret making the offer returned.

7

THE ESPRESSO MAKER HUMMED AS IT WARMED UP AND I POURED water into the reservoir. Duncan sat politely at my dining table with his hands clasped in front of him while he gazed curiously around my apartment, the half-walls of the living room and kitchen making them visible from his spot. The two bedroom doors were closed. Other than dusting and vacuuming now and then, I hadn't disturbed the boys' room since Austin had left. I hoped he would be more prone to visit than Cameron, especially since all his things were still here.

Duncan's gaze lingered on the framed photos on the wall, pictures of the boys in various places around Seattle. Only a couple showed me over the years since I'd usually been the photographer rather than the subject. I'd long since removed all trace of my ex from the picture collection. After Austin had left, I'd dug out an old photo of the first man I'd ever loved—the first *were-wolf* I'd loved—and hung it near a window that looked out onto trees. Even if I hadn't brought Raoul up to my human family, I'd never forgotten him.

"That smells delicious." Duncan nodded to the espresso machine.

"It will be. Now that I only have one mouth to feed, I splurge for the good stuff." I waved to my preferred brand of coffee beans from Italy.

When I'd been clawing my way out of debt, I'd settled for Folger's, but it had been a great relief when I'd paid off the last credit card and gone back to buying fresh espresso beans.

"I'm surprised those delectable aromas don't entice hordes of men to line up at your kitchen window."

"The hordes go to the drive-thru bikini-barista stand down the street."

"That doesn't sound like as refined of an experience."

"You think my apartment and I are refined, huh?" I glanced at the twenty-year-old furniture and chips of laminate gouged out of the countertops.

"Sitting down is civilized. Swilling coffee in one's van is not. And bikinis in this climate are impractical. It's as rainy and dreary here as in England, which I didn't imagine was possible until I came here."

"I'm guessing Seattle baristas have to run heaters in their espresso stands most of the year."

I let the conversation lapse, not practiced at keeping one up. Further, having a man in my apartment felt strange. I hadn't dated or had anyone besides my kids in here since my ex-husband left.

My handful of female friends kept encouraging me to get out and meet new people, but I'd been focused on keeping the boys fed and cared for until recently. Now that they were gone, I could consider going out more, but I'd shifted from worrying about them to worrying about my future. Since I'd never had a retirement plan, that was a concern. Lately, I'd been taking odd jobs on the side and putting money into a special account. Since property management and fixing things around the apartment complex was what I knew, I was saving to buy a small multifamily building of my own, with the hope of the rents bringing in income after I got too old to work. Assuming a werewolf, or the minions of a werewolf, didn't kill me before then.

"Do you want milk in yours? A latte?" I waved toward the frothing wand, then summoned a double shot from the machine.

The espresso maker was the most expensive appliance I owned. Other than my car, it was the most expensive *thing* I owned. One Christmas, it had been a gift from my ex after he'd come into some money and he'd been trying to buy my forgiveness for sleeping around—again. As much as I hated him now—I'd thrown out almost everything in the apartment he'd touched—I hadn't been willing to get rid of the espresso maker. I loved it and the rich dark coffee it produced.

"Nope. I like it straight and strong. Un café allongé. Uhm." Duncan regarded the side of the espresso machine. "Don't take this the wrong way, but is that a, er, phallic symbol on the side of your coffee maker?"

"It was supposed to be a fist holding up a middle finger." I opened a drawer to show him the permanent marker I'd used to draw it. "My artistic skills are lacking, and my sons said it looked like a penis. The next day, the side fingers had been turned into testicles. I'm not sure which of the boys was responsible, but the drawing conveys my feelings toward the person who gave me the machine equally well, so I didn't chastise them."

"Who was the giver?"

"My ex-husband. That drink you said, that's the same as an Americano, right?" I added hot water to the espresso.

"I believe so."

A soft beeping came from the table, and I frowned over at Duncan. He was tinkering with a handheld electronic device. Was that the same tool that he'd aimed toward Bolin's man purse?

Immediately suspicious of him again, I pointed at it. "What is that?"

Duncan waved toward a case he'd brought in with him and set on the table by the door with his keys. I'd thought it was a *camera* case. But it was open now, this little device extracted. Whatever it was, it wasn't a camera.

"My magic detector." Duncan pointed to a small LED display. "It might be able to help you identify the ingredients in your potion."

"I already *know* the ingredients."

Okay, I only knew *some* of them, the ones mentioned on the vials. If only from the color of the liquid, I suspected there were more. It wasn't as if my retired witch-alchemist had created FDA-approved labels with calories, macros, and every ingredient listed.

Maybe the supposed magic detector could help, but I eyed it with as much suspicion as I had for Duncan. I'd never heard of such a device.

I took our two coffees to the table and also grabbed a few squares of a recent chocolate find: Peruvian dark with sea salt and ghost pepper chili. It wasn't as spicy as it sounded, but the sweetness mixed with the saltiness and a slight kick made it fabulous.

"Do you have any remnants of one of your potions?" Duncan asked mildly, nodding his thanks as he accepted the coffee. He picked up one of the chocolate squares and sniffed it. "I can attempt to analyze them."

I leaned closer to eye the supposed magic detector, a little box with crossed antennae that brought to mind a divining rod out of a museum. Duncan either pushed it closer to me, or it pulled his arm in my direction. Either way, it started beeping, its antennae quivering at my chest.

I scowled at it.

"Why, my lady. The device is drawn to you. Are you magical?"

I leaned back and stated, "No," though he and his gists had

already implied he knew the truth. To distract him, I asked, "Are you?"

Duncan turned the device toward his chest. The antennae also quivered at him, and the detector beeped again, more loudly than it had at me. "Goodness."

Smiling, he set it down and sipped from his steaming coffee cup.

Shaking my head, I said, "Stay here," and went into my bedroom.

Glad I'd made my bed that morning, however half-assedly, I padded through to the bathroom to grab the vial. More beeping came from the dining table. No, Duncan had left the table and stood in the doorway to the bedroom, waving that thing around.

"What are you doing? I said stay in the kitchen."

"My apologies, my lady. I *am* trying to obey your wishes, but the device is magical, you see, and it's—" Duncan tugged backward, tendons standing out in his neck as he pulled. Or he did a good job *acting* like he was pulling. "I didn't expect your flat to contain so *much* magic."

He grunted again as it seemed to pull him a step into the bedroom, the antennae pointing toward one ceiling corner and then another. He tugged at it, drawing back to the doorway. The antennae swung about, this time pointing to the floor under one of the nightstands.

What the hell was going on?

"Perhaps we should have analyzed the ingredients outside," Duncan said.

I watched the entire event—the entire *charade*?—with great suspicion. "Turn it off."

"But then we can't—"

"Turn it off!" I yelled.

Or was it almost a roar? My fingers clenched into fists as the same bestirring of my werewolf blood that I'd felt the night before surged through my veins, even closer to surfacing this time. The urge to change was almost overwhelming. I wanted to spring over and destroy that device, then run out into the woods, racing between the trees until I found appropriate game to slay.

I took a deep breath and forced my fingers to unclench. This wasn't a fight, and I didn't need to lose my temper. What I did need was to find someone to make my potion. In a couple more days, when the moon grew full, I might not be able to stop these urges. And I well remembered what could happen when I changed.

"I apologize," Duncan said, dropping the *my lady* and sounding more serious. Thankfully, the beeping had stopped. He'd turned off the device. "Are you okay?"

"I'm fine." I wished he hadn't seen my hands clench, my face contort with barely restrained fury. No, not fury. The call of the wolf.

His face softened with understanding. I looked away. I didn't want empathy or sympathy or whatever he was offering. I wanted my privacy and my humanity back.

"There's no magic in my apartment other than this." I held up the vial, the couple of drops of the potion remaining in the bottom.

"Ah." Duncan glanced toward the ceiling corners. "Of course."

He nodded and returned to the dining table, setting the device on it.

I scowled and didn't move, my gaze shifting to the ceilings. They were painted in unassuming white eggshell, and there was absolutely nothing magical about them. Nothing unusual at all. Nor was there anything odd about the floor under the nightstand.

But...

Was it possible there *was* something magical that I'd somehow forgotten about? I couldn't imagine what. Other than my potions, I'd eschewed all things paranormal after rejecting my werewolf heritage. I didn't hang out with witches, didn't go ghost hunting, and didn't even read books about the supernatural. Nor had I ever invited my alchemist, or anyone else I suspected of magical tendencies, into my apartment.

Still...

"Bring your doohickey back in here, Duncan." I made myself add, "*Please.*"

My ex hadn't appreciated taking orders from a woman. Not many men I'd met did. But sometimes orders slipped out, a vestige of the days when I'd been with my family, a member of the pack and my mother's daughter. She'd been grooming me to be the female alpha, the mate of a male alpha. Had I stayed, I might have helped run the Snohomish Savagers one day.

"My, ah... doohickey?" In the doorway again, Duncan glanced down at his crotch, before snapping his fingers with enlightenment and turning to grab the supposed magic detector.

I scowled again. This guy was turning it into my regular facial expression.

"Sorry," he said. "Americans have so *many* terms for their sex organs that it can be bewildering to newcomers to your land."

"Uh-huh, I'm sure women you barely know invite you to bring your *sex organs* into their bedrooms all the time."

Duncan opened his mouth, a cocky statement probably on his lips, but he considered my scowl and only shrugged. "It's happened on occasion."

I snorted but didn't tell him he was full of himself. He *was* handsome, silvering pelt not withstanding, and he had that European accent that we American girls fall for. Bedroom invitations probably happened *regularly* for him.

"There shouldn't be any magic in the room besides this." I lifted the potion. "Why is your thing beeping at the ceiling and floor?"

"Let's find out." Duncan turned it back on and followed the quivering antennae—the device really *did* appear to be pulling him—to one of the corners. It vacillated between wanting to draw him to the ceiling and to the floor under the nightstand.

I walked around the bed, put the potion vial on my dresser, and shifted the furniture aside. The floor was easier to investigate than the ceiling.

A rug covered vinyl planks designed to look like hardwood boards, an upgrade I'd helped put into a lot of the units over the years, after the owners had gotten tired of replacing carpets whenever there was a turn. I knelt and swept my hand across the planks but didn't feel anything strange. I also peeled back the bottom of the rug and probed under the nightstand.

Duncan stood close, though he stayed far enough to the side so that he wasn't touching me.

I arched my eyebrows up at him. "There's nothing here."

He'd been gazing up at the ceiling, a finger pointing toward what also appeared to be nothing, but he looked down. The metal detector drew his arm until the antennae tapped the vinyl planks in a spot I'd already checked.

"Could there be something *under* the floor?" Duncan asked.

"I helped install this stuff," I said skeptically. "There's definitely nothing between the plywood underfloor and the vinyl planks except adhesive. Under the plywood, there's a crawlspace for the building. There *could* be something there, I suppose, but maintenance people go down there regularly. Shoot, I've been down there as recently as this spring. We put some rat traps down there. I would have noticed something magical sitting on the vapor barrier."

Probably. Did I really know what *something magical* would look like? Unless a golden chalice had been glowing at me from the dark, maybe not.

"There are ducts?" Duncan waved toward a heat vent under the bed's headboard.

"Oh." Duh. I hadn't considered that. But... "Who would have put something in the *ducts*?"

"Who would have put something in your ceiling?" He waved upward.

"Unless you produce a magical artifact of vast and interesting powers, I'm not going to believe anyone did." I eyed his device, still skeptical. Yes, it had beeped at me and at Duncan, but that only proved it knew a werewolf when it saw one.

"I do hate being disbelieved." Duncan handed the device to me. "Let me see what I can find."

As soon as I grasped it, I could feel its pull, its *magic*. It was indeed drawing me toward that spot in the floor, attracted by who knew what.

Duncan moved the lamp off the nightstand and climbed on top of it.

"I have a ladder in the maintenance room. You could have asked." I curled my lip at dried mud on his boots, small flakes now adorning the nightstand.

"I didn't want to delay what could be a monumental discovery of vast importance." He planted his hands on the walls and peered intently at the corner of the ceiling.

"Yeah, such things are found in my bedroom all the time." As I watched, I vacillated between irritation and curiosity. Meanwhile, the magic detector kept its pull on me, not wanting me to lift its antennae from the floor.

"There's a tiny hole here in the corner." Duncan pointed. "And it looks like someone patched a larger one around it. There are paintbrush strokes around it whereas the rest of the wall was done with a roller brush, I believe."

"What? Let me see."

Duncan hopped down from the nightstand, and I surged up on top of it, no longer worried about mud or taking the time to find a ladder. I rose on tiptoes to peer at the spot, wishing the light were better, but trees outside the window kept sun from flowing in, even on days when it was out. Damn, there *was* a little hole.

It was so small I'd never noticed it—how many people looked closely around their bedrooms on a regular basis, anyway? And, yes, he was right about the brush strokes. From the floor, they weren't noticeable, but this close...

"I've never done any repairs here," I said.

"Have your children? Or, did you say you were married?"

"Yeah, but my family has never done any repairs *anywhere*. If anything, they're the reason *I've* needed to do repairs." I remembered Cameron putting a fist through his wall two years earlier when I'd told him the college fund was gone. He'd also been angry then because I'd forbidden Chad from returning. That hadn't been a good time.

"Do you want to get a knife so you can cut into the ceiling?" Duncan offered.

"I'm not going to stab a knife into the drywall like a savage." I climbed down, retrieved my toolbox from under the kitchen sink, and pulled out a small flashlight and a cordless reciprocating saw. After checking the battery, I returned to the nightstand.

"You keep a jab saw in your apartment?" Duncan asked with amusement, picking up the magic detector and thankfully turning it off to stop the beeping.

"It's not weird." I climbed back onto the nightstand. "I'm the handywoman as well as the property manager, remember? You should see all the tools I have in the maintenance shed."

"I didn't say it was weird. I'm tempted to proclaim that a woman with power tools is sexy, but you're in a good position to kick me in the face." He smirked up at me.

"I wouldn't do that." I thumbed the saw on to enlarge the hole in the ceiling.

"Because you've seen me fight and respect my ability to defend myself?"

I *had* seen him fight, and he absolutely kicked ass. What I said was, "If I give you a concussion, there might be brain damage, and you'd never be able to move your van out of my parking lot."

"That *would* be an inconvenience."

"A tremendous one, yes."

Duncan knelt and peered behind the headboard, eyeing the heat vent.

Once I'd cut a hole in the ceiling, I probed the opening with the flashlight. Something glinted, and a twinge of anxiety swept through my gut. There *was* something in there. A small device?

Using the blade, I attempted to wedge it out, but it was attached to something. A cord? A *power supply*? And was that a glass lens?

I managed to maneuver the device out enough to grab it between thumb and forefinger, then yanked. It snapped free of the cord, and I found myself staring at a tiny camera.

Someone had been spying on me in my bedroom?

It had grown quiet, and I could *feel* my heart hammering, reverberating against my eardrums.

Duncan regarded my find. "That's creepy."

"No shit."

8

WITH FURY AND FEAR FLOODING ME WITH ADRENALINE, I DROPPED the tiny camera onto the nightstand under my feet and stomped on it to break it. I wished I could also break the neck of whatever creep had planted it.

On the third stomp, a tiny snap sounded. White light flashed, and a pulse of magical energy surged up my leg, pitching me backward. I tumbled off the nightstand and struck the wall.

Duncan sprang forward and caught me before I pitched to the floor. I groaned, belatedly remembering that his magic detector had alerted us to the device, meaning it hadn't come out of a box from RadioShack.

After mumbling a thank-you, I wriggled free from his grip. I resolutely grabbed my saw and walked around the bed toward the other corner.

"Do you have any idea who would want to spy on you?" Duncan asked.

"No." As I shoved the other nightstand into the corner, I thought of my werewolf family, the cousin I hadn't yet called. But there was no reason the pack would want to spy on me. And certainly not in my *bedroom*. That was what made this extra creepy. How often had I wandered naked from the shower out to the dresser to grab clothes? And when my husband had been here, we'd had sex right under those cameras. If they'd been there that long. Had they? "I don't suppose your device can tell me *when* these were installed?"

"No. Sorry." Duncan's voice came from the floor. He'd pushed the bed back and knelt so he could remove the vent cover.

"Do you mind?"

"Helping you? Not at all."

"Do you mind not *snooping* right in front of me? If there's any searching to do, *I'll* do it." After finding the camera, I dreaded learning what might be down in the heat duct. Already, I wasn't sure I wanted a witness for this. Duncan probably thought I was a deviant, or had *dated* deviants, someone who'd put this stuff up there.

But who did I know who would have had access to my apartment? *And* who knew where to acquire magical items? I'd never even heard of magical cameras. Where did one go to buy them? An alchemist with an electronics background?

"Of course, my lady." Duncan rose, lifting his hands. "I'm merely trying to be helpful. And I'm always curious. I admitted that, didn't I?"

"Just... write down whatever you need to know about that potion, okay? That would be helpful. I need to find someone to make it before..." Before the full moon, I thought but didn't say. "Just before."

Duncan watched me as I lifted the saw to drill another hole. "May I ask a question?"

"No."

"Ah."

Something told me he wanted to know *why* I took the potions instead of embracing my heritage, my heritage that could turn me into an animal with the power to kill. The distressingly *easy* power to kill.

"Potion, then. Right." Duncan turned toward the dresser.

I drilled the hole and found another camera plugged in above the ceiling, its power cord running who knew where. Again, I yanked it out, snapping the connection. I was tempted to stomp on it to destroy it, hardly caring if the magic knocked me on my ass again, but it was probably a good idea to leave it intact and try to figure out where it was transmitting. Was it hooked up to my Wi-Fi? Or someone else's Wi-Fi? There were dozens of networks in the apartment complex, and I never would have noticed if another had appeared. Nor was I a techy person who would have noticed if a foreign device was using mine. Did these cameras even *need* a network? Maybe the magic allowed them to magically transmit the feed to...

To where?

"I wonder if Chad did it," I muttered, staring at the device in my palm.

He was a mundane human, but he'd always been interested in magic, and he might have figured out where to buy such a thing. But why would he have cared about spying on me after he left? Out of jealousy? To make sure I didn't hook up with another guy?

He'd been hooking up with women left and right, so that would be hypocrisy, but I wouldn't put it past him. When we'd been together, he'd snapped at other men who'd flirted or even looked too long at me. That might even have been the reason I'd stopped wearing makeup and dressing in anything that showed off skin or curves. To make those incidents less likely to occur.

"Is Chad your husband?" Duncan had the potion vial up, squinting at the label.

"My *ex*-husband."

"How long ago did he leave?"

"He didn't *leave*. I kicked the cheating bastard out. If he'd had his way, he would have kept returning from his *business trips* to shag me in between screwing every bimbo along the way, including that blonde girl he's yachting around the world with now. Assuming she hasn't gotten sick of him and kicked him out. *He* never had money for a boat. I know that's her yacht."

Duncan looked up, his lips parting. With surprise? Sympathy?

"I'm sorry. That must have been rough on you. And your kids." He nodded toward the photos of them on the wall.

I snapped my jaw shut. I hadn't meant to let that rant out and reveal so much of my personal life to a stranger.

"He's been gone for almost three years," I said, answering his earlier question. "You think the magic in these could have worked and been transmitting for that long?"

"Yes."

"Is there any way to tell where they were transmitting?"

Duncan hesitated. "There might be, but it's beyond my knowledge. We'd have to find an expert. I can ask my contacts or the local alchemist when I give her the information on this." He held up the potion. "It's helpful that some of the ingredients are written on the label. Gardenia oil, dried snakeskin, banana slug slime, birch bark, and blood of the natterjack toad. Must be a tasty tincture."

"I shove chocolate in my mouth after swallowing it."

"Understandable."

Duncan picked up a tube on the dresser. Hell, was that my estradiol cream? I hadn't expected visitors, so I hadn't tidied up.

"What's this?" he asked. "Another potion?"

"No." I winced. "Put that down. Or in the drawer, please." I hopped down from the nightstand to grab it from him.

He started to obey, pulling out the drawer, but he also read the label. That prompted him to squawk and drop it on the floor.

I rolled my eyes. "Really, dude? The slug slime and toad blood didn't bother you, but the hormone cream made you shriek?"

"No. Yes." Duncan lifted his hands and backed into the doorway, as if he'd dropped a viper and it was slithering after him. "It wasn't a *shriek*. I just didn't realize... I mean, I knew women did things for... *things,* but I thought it was when they were older. You seem, you know. Healthy. And, uhm. Vibrant." He looked me up and down.

"I *am* healthy and vibrant. I'm just of an age where the hormones are fluctuating."

"The, uhm, your blood doesn't... keep you and your parts all... fit?"

Not when I took a potion to dull the wolf, no. Was werewolf blood even supposed to change anything about female hormones? I could have asked my mother if we'd spoken in the last decade...

"Just finish writing down the potion ingredients, please," I told him.

"Yes, of course." Duncan took his magic detector and the vial out to the table.

Well, I'd found a way to keep guys out of my bedroom at least. Snorting, I put the tube in the drawer. I tucked the camera in the drawer too, stuffing it in a sock so that it wouldn't see anything until I could find an expert to examine it.

"Are you going to check the duct?" Duncan asked.

"Maybe later."

In *private*, I didn't say. A part of me wanted to leave it be, but what if the person or people who'd put the cameras in my bedroom figured out I'd found them? And what if that prompted them to activate whatever else was in there? Some Plan B. Maybe I could sleep in my sons' room for a while...

"It's none of my business, of course," Duncan said while he wrote down ingredients, "but the cameras seem a little malevolent."

"Tell me about it."

"If you unearth a dangerous artifact, it could have defenses that'll do more than knock you back. You might want someone here in case things go wrong."

Not a bad point, but I didn't want to have to trust a stranger—a stranger who might have ulterior motives—to call an ambulance for me. Who *could* I trust?

I had friends that I'd made during my years living as a normal human, but they didn't know anything about the paranormal. If I tried to explain this, they would think I was insane. The same held true for the tenants, especially since my alchemist lady had disappeared. I was on friendly terms with a lot of the long-term residents here, but you were supposed to ask neighbors for a cup of sugar, not to call 9-1-1 if a magical artifact kicked your ass.

Maybe I could have Bolin stand by. He knew about magic, and, even if I barely knew him, I'd worked for his parents forever. That meant I knew a lot more about him than I did about Duncan.

But... Duncan was here. And I might need that magic detector to figure out the exact location of the whatever it was.

I sighed. "I doubt anyone put a dangerous artifact in my heat duct, but if you want to stay, fine."

"Okay." Duncan rose from his chair and stepped toward the bedroom, but he glanced warily at the dresser before crossing the threshold.

"I put the cream away. I didn't want to hear you shriek again."

Duncan squinted at me. "I'm feeling the urge to do something strong and fierce to remind you that I'm quite manly."

"If you want, I can find something heavy for you to carry for me later." I pushed the bed frame farther away from the wall.

"That might do it. Something made from metal and spikes."

"I've got three kinds of rakes if you want to tackle the leaves outside." I waved out the window toward the autumn foliage scattering the lawn.

"Hm. Would you consider such an activity manly?"

"*Extremely.*" I knelt to remove the vent cover. "Sexy too." I waggled my eyebrows at him, deciding that if I succeeded at inveigling him into doing yard work, I would offer him free parking for the rest of the week.

"Would you want me to do it shirtless?"

"That's optional, though Grammy Tootie in C-3 would have her nose pressed to the window watching. I always catch her sneaking peeks at our contractors."

"I'd be more interested in *your* nose against the window."

"My nose is distracted right now." With the vent cover removed, I dropped to my belly and lowered my flashlight into the hole. Of course, the duct immediately turned a corner, so I couldn't see to the spot the magic detector had liked. The duct *did* look like it headed in the right direction to go past it. "I don't see anything glowing," I offered.

"I wouldn't think whoever placed the item would have chosen that location if unexpected illumination might have seeped through the vent and alerted you to its presence."

"I don't spend a lot of time looking under the bed for strange glows coming from the ducts," I said, but he was right. I *would* have noticed something like that at night with the lights out. "I can't imagine why there would even be something down there."

"Because it's a good hiding spot," Duncan said with certainty. And a little excitement. Because he had the heart of a treasure hunter? Probably. "I doubt whoever put the cameras up there anticipated someone cruising through your apartment with a magic detector."

"With reason."

I twisted to poke my arm into the duct, deciding I was glad I wasn't alone. I might never admit it aloud, but the entire situation creeped me out. Images came to mind of rats and snakes and more inimical things lurking around the corner of the duct.

My phone rang in my pocket. One-handedly, I toggled it to silence without looking at the screen.

"I should have made you do this." I patted about, shifting so I could extend my arm deeper and trying not to think about getting stuck. "To prove your manliness."

"That is more in line with my special abilities than wielding a rake. If there's anything metal on whatever it is, I could get my magnet to slide down there."

"We can try that if—" My knuckles brushed something, and a zing shot up my arm.

I drew back, hesitant. It hadn't exactly hurt, but it had seemed like a warning. Like maybe if I offended whatever it was, it *would* hurt me. Further, I wasn't sure if I could reach deep enough to grab it fully. Had it felt metal? Magnetic? Maybe. It had been cool.

"Did you find something?" Duncan knelt close, looking at the vent and my face intently, eagerly.

"Yeah." I eyed him.

The intentness was such a contrast to his usual affable smiles that it was unsettling. Was it possible he had *expected* to find something odd in my apartment? I didn't see how, as this was beyond puzzling to me, but he'd brought that magic detector in. And, despite his comments about analyzing my potion, he'd yet to swing the device over it. Could it *really* analyze alchemical ingredients?

"Can you get it?" Duncan asked. "Do you want me to try?"

I started to say *no*, but I doubted I could reach it. I would have to go down to the crawlspace and cut into the duct from below. Then I would have to later repair the duct.

"Go ahead and try." I drew my arm back. "But it zapped me, so be careful."

"You'd be distressed if magic sizzled up my arm and blackened my handsome features?"

"I'd be distressed if I had to explain to the police why there was a dead werewolf on my bedroom floor." I raised frank eyebrows as I shifted away from the duct. It had felt daring saying that, and I was curious what his reaction would be. He knew I was a werewolf, and I knew he was a werewolf, but it was the first either of us had spoken the word.

Duncan didn't show signs of surprise, only taking my place on the floor. "You can tell them we were having sex, and your great beauty and vigor roused me to such a frenetic extent that I had a heart attack."

"There's no way I'm saying that for a police report." After thinking for a moment, I added, "I'd probably put gloves on and roll you out into the woods."

He laughed as he slid his arm into the duct. From the awkward position, he met my eyes. "You're a more interesting person than I expected."

"You expected to meet me when you showed up in the woods next door?"

"Well, no. When I first saw you, I thought you were pretty, but I didn't imagine you having, you know, personality." He winked at me, but he looked a little flustered.

"You didn't think someone carrying a toilet across the parking lot would have personality?"

He laughed again. "I suppose I should have."

Something about his comments seemed off—had he expected to meet me *before* he'd arrived to metal detect out there? I was about to probe further, but his eyes lit with excitement.

"Ah! I've got—" He jerked his arm back, delight turning to pain as he gasped and winced. "Something that does indeed defend itself."

"I'll get my oven mitts." I headed for the kitchen.

"To roll my body out to the woods?"

"To insulate your hands, in case it helps." I had no idea if padded mitts could protect one from magical zaps, but they couldn't hurt.

When I returned, Duncan had pulled his arm out of the duct

and fished a small tin out of his pocket. It was the kind of thing lip balm came in, but the contents glowed a faint violet. He rubbed some over his hand, held up a finger, then slid his arm back into the duct.

"You came prepared." I laid the mitts on the dresser.

"You never know when a little anti-magic cream will come in handy."

"Uh-huh." I had a feeling my first hunch about Duncan had been correct, that I was right to be suspicious of him. "What'd you say you were looking for in the woods over there?"

"Treasures."

"I think you're full of shit, Duncan Calderwood."

"I'm touched that you remember my name. Your attentive interest makes me want to fulfill your every desire later."

"You can start with the raking."

"Shirtlessly, yes."

"That's *your* choice."

He shifted his arm deeper. "Got it."

He grimaced but didn't wince as deeply as before as he pulled his arm out. He held a weathered ivory case about six inches long and four inches wide, with decorative vines, leaves, and flowers carved on all the sides except the top. The lid held a wolf with its snout tilted toward the moon, its jaws parted to reveal its long, sharp teeth.

A chill went through me, the certainty that it wasn't an accident that the case had been hidden in my apartment. But by whom? And when?

I'd been in this apartment for more than twenty years. The building was decades older than that, but the ducts had been cleaned four or five years back. If the case had been there then, it would have been discovered by a bewildered HVAC technician.

Chad was the only person I could imagine who might have stashed something in here during that time frame, but where would he have gotten a magical case? And why choose some-thing with a wolf on top? He'd always been into werewolves, but he hadn't collected lupine tchotchkes, as far as I knew, when we'd been married. This was more than a *tchotchke*, but it was easier imagining it appealing to my kind than a mundane human.

Could someone in my family have come by when I'd been gone and tucked the case into the vent for safekeeping? In a place where the rest of the pack wouldn't look? It could make sense. Since I'd ostracized myself, my family members probably didn't spend any time thinking about me—or my apartment.

Using the hand he'd rubbed the cream on, Duncan tried to open the silver clasp, but there was a tiny lock that kept it fastened. He attempted to wiggle the lid free. Nothing happened.

"Hm." He turned the case about, examining the hinges. They also appeared to be made from silver. "It looks old, but it's quite sturdy. And probably reinforced with magic. I guess I won't ask you to stomp on it to open it."

"I only stomp on things to destroy them. That's beautiful. It belongs on an ornate fireplace mantel."

"Don't you want to find out what's inside?" Judging from the way he turned it all about, *he* wanted that. "I hear something clunking around in there."

I squinted at him, wondering if this was what he'd come for. He'd mentioned that people hired him to find things. Had someone known about this object and done exactly that?

"Not if it involves being zapped," I said.

Still holding the case, almost cradling it to his chest with love, Duncan rose. "Do you want me to take it to the alchemist and see if—"

"No." I grabbed an oven mitt and plucked the case from his grip, certain that if he walked out with it, I would never see him or *it* again. If he disappeared from my life, I wouldn't tear up, but I was interested in finding out what the case was and why someone had been monitoring my bedroom with cameras.

"You're certain?"

"I am." In my grip, the case sizzled a magical protest, my oven mitt not as useful as his magical goo, but I gritted my teeth and endured the pain.

"What are you going to do with it?"

"I don't know yet." With him watching, I nestled it in the top drawer of my dresser, next to the sock with the camera. I smirked and put the tube of hormone cream over it.

He snorted. "You want to make sure I don't come back for it, don't you?"

"Absolutely." I narrowed my eyes as I regarded him. "If you linger around the premises, it had better be to rake the lawn."

His eyes narrowed in return, a challenge in them. Or maybe that was *calculation*. Was I going to have to guard that case to keep him from sneaking back to get it?

"I did agree to that task, didn't I?" Duncan asked, making me regret that I'd suggested it.

If I hadn't, he wouldn't have an excuse to stick around. Still, it might be better to *know* where he was than *wonder* where he was.

"You did," I said. "You wanted to show off your manliness and were excited by the prospect of Grammy Tootie watching."

"Oh yeah. That got my engine revved up."

Duncan returned to the table and tucked the vial and list of ingredients he'd written into his pocket. He started for the door but paused to look thoughtfully back at me. "You said the rake is in your maintenance shed?"

"*Three* rakes are in there. Take your pick."

"I will." Before heading for the door, he removed his shirt and tossed it on the back of a chair.

Lean and muscular, with a few old scars, he was as fit as I'd imagined after seeing him fight. I kept my face neutral and folded my arms over my chest, refusing to give him the satisfaction of seeing me ogle his torso. My gaze *did* snag on ropy scars around each of his wrists. Those had to have a story.

At the door, he halted abruptly before opening it. With an odd note in his voice, he asked, "Were you expecting company?"

"No."

Someone outside knocked, fist thumping the door with the subtlety of a battering ram.

"It's a werewolf," Duncan said quietly.

Fresh unease swept through me, and I pulled out my phone with a mix of dread and certainty to see who'd called earlier. My cousin Augustus.

9

I STEPPED TOWARD THE WINDOW, SURPRISED TO SEE THAT NIGHT HAD fallen and intending to find out who was knocking before I answered. But Duncan opened the door first. He was still shirtless, and the eyes of the man on the threshold widened. No, not the *man* on the threshold. The werewolf.

Oh, he looked human—broad-shouldered and in his late thirties with a Starter jacket, ripped jeans, and slicked-back black hair —but I was close enough now to sense him, the same as Duncan had. And, after a moment, I recognized him, though I hadn't seen him in decades. Cousin Augustus was one of six sons and daughters my mother's sister had birthed. Long ago, I'd been his babysitter.

"Who are you?" Augustus asked Duncan, his shoulders bunching under his jacket, his muscles straining against the sleeves.

"I'm here servicing Luna's needs." Duncan lifted a hand to the doorframe, flexing his biceps in the process.

"He isn't servicing anything but the lawn," I called over his shoulder, then tapped Duncan, wanting him to let me past.

Augustus didn't bristle any less at the announcement and continued to glare at Duncan. It didn't help that Duncan didn't move to make things easy for me. I had to duck to slip out under his arm. Duncan stepped out with me and stood at my side as I faced my cousin.

"You're here a lot, *lawn* boy," Augustus said.

He was more than a decade younger than Duncan, so using *boy* was nothing but insulting. Not that Duncan wasn't goofy and boyish most of the time, but Augustus wouldn't know about that.

Nothing in Duncan's cool expression was youthful or naive now. He gazed back without sign of intimidation, though Augustus stood several inches taller than he and had filled out like a refrigerator since last I'd seen him. A very muscled refrigerator.

"It's a big lawn," Duncan said.

"What can I do for you, Augie?" I suspected the childhood nickname might make him bristle but wanted to remind him of a time when I'd been in charge of him.

He finally shifted his gaze to me, though he maintained a tense and wary stance, fingers ready to snap into fists, and he kept Duncan in his sights. "You didn't answer my call."

"You haven't called for more than a decade. I assumed you butt-dialed me."

Augustus mouthed the word, "*Butt*," then shook his head. "I left a message asking you to meet me at Echo Lake Park last night. It's important."

"Sorry. I've been busy and haven't checked my messages."

"*Busy*. With the lawn boy."

"No," I said, but Duncan spoke over me.

"We had a *fabulous* dinner together last night. Except for being attacked by a pack of wolves and stray dogs. You wouldn't know anything about that, would you?"

Even though it had crossed my mind that Augustus or someone else in the pack might have been connected to the attack,

Duncan's accusation surprised me. After all, he'd just *met* my cousin. He couldn't know anything about my family's dynamics. Or so I assumed. His eyes were slits as he regarded Augustus, as if he already knew the answer.

"Luna is my cousin," Augustus said. "I have no reason to attack her."

"Or have minions attack her?"

"No. *You*, on the other paw... Who the hell are you? This is Snohomish Savager territory. You came on our turf without asking permission or bringing an offering. There aren't many wolves in this area anymore. I would have heard about it if you'd visited our alpha. *I* keep in close communication with the family." Augustus gave me a scathing look.

"You know why I don't communicate with them," I said quietly. "No, why *they* don't communicate with *me*."

When I'd left the pack, I'd been running from my own demons, not spurning the family. Once, I'd gone back long enough to explain it to my mother, but she hadn't understood. And, going by the years of silence since then, she still didn't understand. My *family* had cut ties with me, not the other way.

"Because you've turned *human*," Augustus said as if that were the most egregious crime in the world. "You don't hunt, you don't change, you don't heed the call, and you smell like them. You're *weak* like them. It's *disgusting*."

Duncan took a step forward, as if he might spring at Augustus to defend me.

I held up a hand, not wanting him to get involved. Even though I didn't trust him and doubted he had my best interests in mind, I didn't want him picking a fight with the pack. That was a good way for a lone wolf to get killed. If Duncan hurt Augustus, the entire family would hunt him down. More werewolves than Augustus might be in the area right now. The rest of my cousins and some of my half-brothers could be lurking in the woods.

"Not that it's any of your business," I told Augustus, "but I did it for a reason."

He sneered. "So you could mate with a weakling human and spawn feeble human offspring."

"I'm so delighted you've been keeping tabs on me." I thought of the cameras.

"Your *mother* keeps tabs. And your aunt. Only they care, and I don't know why. Your mother has other offspring, offspring *loyal* to the pack, and you— you are dead to the rest of us."

"So... you came to chat up a ghost?"

"I came because *you* didn't show up at the park."

"What would have happened if I had? What do you want?"

"To *talk*."

I resisted the urge to point out that the conversational skills he was displaying wouldn't make anyone eager to show up to chat with him. I didn't need to go out of my way to insult him. His words, *you are dead to the rest of us*, were chilling. I'd had suspicions but hadn't fully realized the family had been that deeply affronted by my choice. What if it was only because of my mother that the pack hadn't done *more* than ignore me these past decades? She wouldn't live forever. What then?

"I'm here, and you're here." I shrugged. "Talk now."

"It's a private matter. Send the lawn boy away."

Duncan didn't budge.

This wasn't any of his business, and I would have preferred *not* to have an outsider witness me arguing with a family member, but Augustus's eyes held a dangerous glint. If he *had* been the were-wolf howling the night before, and he *had* sent those four-legged minions, that meant he either wanted me wounded or dead. Conversing alone with him could be a bad idea.

"Just tell me what you want, Augustus," I said. "Duncan is only visiting and doesn't have a pack of his own. It's not like he's going to gossip about our family to his kin."

Duncan's face twisted in a quick pained wince before he recovered, putting his insouciant mask back on. My words had only been a guess, and I hadn't meant to offend him, so I winced myself. I should have known that a lone wolf might have a troubled past. Few left their packs of their own accord. Usually, they had to depart because they'd challenged an alpha and lost or because they'd been ostracized for other reasons.

Augustus's nostrils twitched as he looked past us and into my apartment. What he was smelling besides the lingering aroma of coffee, I didn't know, but his senses were keener than mine.

"Send him away, and let's go inside," Augustus said, meeting my gaze. "You *will* speak with me."

He lifted a hand, as if to push me back into the apartment.

I tensed, ready to attack the bastard, however suicidal it might be. But Duncan sprang first, blocking him.

My cousin turned on him, grabbing for his throat. Duncan ducked the snatch and bowled into Augustus. They crashed to the ground, rolling and grabbing and snarling like the wolves they could be. Like they would *become* if this escalated.

"Augustus, stop!" I blurted, not wanting Duncan to be hurt because of me. "I'll talk to you."

But the men didn't listen. Maybe they didn't even hear me.

I ran inside and opened my toolkit, grabbing the largest wrench I had.

"A proper property manager should pack heat," I grumbled, running back to the doorway.

For twenty years, I'd never felt the need to own a weapon in Shoreline, but the last two days had brought biker gangs, an enraged cousin, and magically controlled strays. It might be time to rethink that choice.

Wrench raised, I sprang onto the walkway. A loud snarl rang out, a *lupine* snarl.

Two wolves snapped and writhed on the lawn in front of my door. Savage snarls and growls emanated from the fight.

The combatants were huge, a dark-gray wolf that had to be Augustus and his salt-and-pepper furred aggressor—Duncan. Though Duncan was older, he was as heavily muscled as Augustus and just as large. Maybe larger. As men, they hadn't been the same size, but more powerful magic sometimes created a larger and more powerful wolf. Duncan was the one driving my cousin back, using speed and strength to his advantage. Already, a gash in the gray wolf's shoulder had spattered blood onto the walkway.

Someone in an upstairs apartment screamed.

I winced. Of *course* there would be witnesses.

The noise startled Duncan more than Augustus, and my cousin took advantage. He charged, bowling into the bigger wolf, and they tumbled into a rhododendron. Leaves flew, and branches snapped.

"Hey! I'm the landscaper, you idiots." I raised the wrench but had no idea how to break up the fight.

Neither wolf glanced at me nor looked up again as a woman in an upstairs apartment yelled at someone to call Animal Control.

Yeah, that would work.

Duncan and Augustus rolled about in the grass, fangs blurring as they snapped for each other's throats. Before long, Duncan recovered from his surprise and came out on top. Standing over Augustus, he lunged for my cousin's throat. Augustus twisted enough to take the bite on the shoulder instead but yelped in pain as the salt-and-pepper wolf tore out a piece of flesh. Duncan shook his lupine head, like a hound that had caught a rabbit. More blood flew, spattering the walkway again as well as the siding and door.

I should have been disgusted, but witnessing the battle and the savagery of wild animals called to the wild in *me*. My blood tingled in my veins as a fierce urge to not only stop the fight but *help* came to me. Whether the wolf in me wanted me to assist Duncan or my own family member, I wasn't sure, but I swore, afraid the magic I'd kept sublimated for so long would rise. My wolf might feel territorial toward the complex I'd lived in for so long and kill *both* of them.

Two angry howls came from the greenbelt, startling me. Who else was out there?

Augustus whined and rolled under the rhododendron to escape Duncan. He was only successful because Duncan paused to look toward the woods. Whoever had howled wasn't visible, but the two wolves sounded close. More of my cousins, as I'd been thinking earlier? I didn't know.

Augustus surged to his feet and snarled, his fear fading. Yes, those had to be allies of his. Back stiff, tail straight, and head up, he looked a lot more confident, despite blood dripping from numerous wounds.

He ran across the lawn, not toward Duncan but toward me. His eyes blazed with the savage determination of a wolf on a mission. A mission to *kill* me.

Though I had no idea why he wanted that, I had little doubt in that moment that he did.

I backed into the doorway, so the frame would guard my flanks, and lifted my wrench. My blood burned hot in my veins, and my skin prickled all over my body. Damn it, I *was* about to change.

But Duncan crashed into Augustus, knocking him off his trajectory. The gray wolf came so close that I could feel his hot slavering breath on my skin. When I swung my wrench, I connected. It struck Augustus in the side of the head right before Duncan took him to the ground.

Standing over my cousin, the advantage all his, Duncan might have delivered a killing blow, but two more large wolves charged across the lawn toward us. They snarled, their cold eyes locked on him.

He'd been an equal for Augustus, but he couldn't win against three. Duncan must have realized that, even with the savagery of werewolf instincts hazing his thoughts, because when he looked at them, he sprang off Augustus and ran.

The pair veered after him with murder in their eyes. Even if Duncan hadn't been hurting Augustus, they would have gone after a lone wolf for intruding upon the pack's territory. But this was especially egregious.

I stepped back onto the walkway and threw my wrench at one of them. If I could buy Duncan some time, he could get away, change, and make it back to his van and drive off. At this rate, I might have to go with him.

My wrench struck one of the wolves in the shoulder. It was a heavy tool, but it wasn't enough to deter him. The pair continued after Duncan, who raced through the apartment complex, rounded one building, and headed out toward the woods.

Still in his lupine form, Augustus groaned. Blood pooled on the walkway under him, but werewolves were notorious for shrugging off pain when they were on the hunt or in battle. Or trying to kill a family member? I had no idea, but I ran inside and grabbed the largest butcher knife in my block.

When I returned to the doorway, the weapon gripped tightly in my hand, Augustus had risen to his feet. After glancing dismissively at the knife, he glared at me and prowled forward. He limped, but he kept coming.

Heart pounding, I raised the blade. "It'll hurt a lot more than the wrench, you betraying bastard."

My blood still surged hot, and I could feel the wolf trying to come out. If the potion hadn't lingered in my veins, I suspected I would already have turned.

The dark-gray wolf paused, nostrils twitching. Sampling the air? No, he was sniffing me.

His eyes closed to slits as he considered me for a long moment before snarling in frustration, then running into the grass. With his wound making his gait uneven, he loped off in the direction the others had gone. To help his allies with Duncan, I had no doubt.

I lowered the knife, at a loss for how to keep my family from killing Duncan. I wished I'd been able to buy him time. Would he be fast enough to outrun those two wolves? Two *fresh* wolves who'd just arrived and weren't injured or tired from the fight?

I didn't know.

10

SHORT BARKS REVERBERATED FROM THE GREENBELT, RISING OVER THE rumble of freeway traffic. They were the vocalizations of wolves hot on the heels of their prey, wolves confident that they would capture and take *down* their prey.

Frustration bubbled within me, and I regretted that I hadn't let the magic take hold and change me. If I'd joined Duncan, we might have been able to fight off my relatives. Two against three could have been doable, especially since Augustus was already injured.

But, with the immediate personal threat past, my blood had cooled, and I no longer felt the tingle of lupine power. In the old days, with the full moon so near, I could have summoned the wolf at will, but the magic would have had to overcome the lingering effects of my last dose of the potion. It had *mostly* but not entirely worn off.

A cry of pain wafted out of the woods. Duncan?

I slammed the butcher knife down on the table by the door, wishing I had a rifle. The power of the slam made Duncan's keys tremble, almost sliding to the floor. I'd forgotten he'd left them and the case for his magic detector by the door. His van had those huge tires. Could it handle driving off road? Maybe there was a gun or other decent weapon inside too, something I could use to help him.

My stomach churned at the idea of attacking my own family—and the repercussions that might result—but they'd started it. My cousin had been trying to *kill* me.

I snatched up the keys and ran toward the parking lot, ignoring a tenant leaning over the balcony railing above. As she looked toward the woods, she spoke rapidly into her phone. Talking to Animal Control, no doubt. I hoped they would tell her to call back the next day during office hours.

The van door wasn't locked, and I sprang into the driver's seat. The first key I tried turned in the ignition, and the Roadtrek roared to life.

I drove straight at the curb. The big tires cheerfully rolled over it and across the sidewalk and into the grass. I headed toward a trail that led into the woods, a dog-poop station and garbage can next to it. I knew the paths through the greenbelt well; what I didn't know was if the van would fit on any but the main route through the center. Even on that one, the branches would hit the sides; they might block the way entirely.

"I just have to get close," I muttered, finding the headlights.

If I could throw open the side door and yell at Duncan to jump inside, we could drive off. Even a magical wolf couldn't keep up with an automobile, not once we got out on the paved streets.

The headlamp beams slashed into the woods, highlighting autumn leaves and dried needles on the ground and moss dangling from bare branches. They also caught a dark-gray wolf crouched between two firs in the distance. A pair of eyes turned toward me, shining an eerie red as they reflected the headlights. Augustus.

I drove toward him, but he darted into the brush and out of view.

As I'd predicted, the branches scraped at the sides of the van, the awful noise making me cringe. Hopefully, the old Roadtrek could take a few hits.

A dark lump to the side of the trail prompted me to lift up off the accelerator. Had they already gotten Duncan?

No, it was a solid gray wolf, one of the two males who'd run across the lawn. He wasn't moving. Was he dead?

I swallowed, thoughts of repercussions again coming to mind.

As I slowed the van, the wolf lifted his head. Okay, not dead. Good.

Injured, he pushed himself to his paws. I tensed, worried he would attack the van, but he shambled away from the trail. Accusing eyes looked back at me before he disappeared from view. I was fairly certain that was another cousin that I hadn't seen since our youth.

I drove further, turning onto a side path that wasn't large enough for a vehicle. But it was in the direction Augustus had gone.

Wood snapped as the van broke branches, the headlight beams wobbling wildly as I drove over roots that tilted them left and right. The big tires flattened a fern, then rolled into a hole that almost kept me from continuing. I pushed on the accelerator, and the engine groaned as it climbed out.

I was contemplating retreating back to the main path when a huge cedar came into view. Duncan, still in his wolf form, had his rump to the tree, his hackles up as he snapped at Augustus and a lighter-gray wolf with a black tip on his tail. Augustus was injured, but the other wolf wasn't.

He leaped in, snapping his jaws at Duncan, then skittered back to Augustus's side before Duncan could retaliate. He couldn't fight both at once. And, damn it, was he injured too? Yes, he slumped back against the cedar, and I could make out deep bloody gashes in his side where fangs had raked him like claws.

His uninjured attacker glanced toward the van, sharp teeth bared, annoyance flashing in golden eyes. Despite my approach, the wolf sprang at Duncan again. Trying to finish him off before help arrived?

I stomped on the accelerator. It startled Augustus, and he looked back, then slid sideways a few steps.

The van hit a root, and I almost pitched out of the seat. I cranked the wheel hard to avoid veering into a tree. Branches slapped the windshield, evergreen needles flying.

Duncan, left facing only one enemy, and perhaps not as injured as he'd led them—and me—to believe, leaped out to meet the gray wolf's charge. They butted chests as their jaws snapped toward each other's throats. Duncan must have weighed more, or put more behind his charge, because he knocked his foe back. The gray wolf bumped against a tree trunk, then stumbled into the path of the van. I accelerated.

The wolf heard the engine and knew I was coming. He crouched to spring away, but I clipped him. He didn't cry out in pain, but I felt the thud as the fender rammed him. He flew, rolling through the ferns before getting his paws under him.

After a glare at me and then Duncan, the gray wolf ran off into the night. Augustus had already disappeared. I glanced in the side mirrors, looking for the injured wolf I'd passed on the way in, but he'd slunk off too.

Relieved, I turned off the van and slid out. The windshield hadn't cracked under the branch assault, but I'd put the giant tires to the test. Snapped twigs, needles, and leaves stuck out of every vent and crack, and fur and blood darkened the fender.

Still in his wolf form, Duncan slumped against the cedar, then collapsed completely, legs crumpling underneath him. Maybe he hadn't been feigning his injuries after all. He'd simply gathered himself for a last charge.

I rushed to his side and knelt, resting a hand on his back, careful to avoid his wounds. In addition to the gashes, one of his pointed ears was ripped, and blood dribbled from a split lip.

"Are you okay?" I knew from experience that he would understand me, but the words would take longer to process when his animal instincts were in control. Duncan would hear them, as if through a haze. "Do you want me to take you to... uhm, the vet?"

It was a dumb question, and he leveled a frank look at me. I almost laughed, imagining him saying something indignant and adding *my lady* to the end.

His gaze shifted toward the van.

"I hope you don't mind that I borrowed your keys. I thought it would be a better weapon than anything in my toolkit."

Duncan lowered his head between his paws, his eyes closing. I didn't think his injuries were grave enough that I needed to worry about him dying, but I did want to get him back to my apartment for a better look. With the battle past, his magic ought to fade soon. He would turn back into his human form.

"You can rest now," I said softly and stroked his thick fur.

Though he'd closed his eyes, he was still conscious, and he leaned into my touch. When his weight settled against me, it almost knocked me over. As I'd noticed before, he was large, even for a werewolf. My family had been foolish to start a fight with him around. Maybe they hadn't realized he would jump to my defense. *I* hadn't realized that.

"Thank you for your help, Duncan. I'm not sure why you helped, but..." I looked off into the dark woods. The pack had disappeared, but I imagined I could still see Augustus's hard eyes, the determination in them, the desire to kill me. *Why* he wanted me dead after all these years, I didn't know, but I didn't doubt that he did. "I'm not sure why you helped," I repeated, still stroking Duncan's back, "but it's clear that you did."

He sighed with contentment at the strokes, now seeming more like a hound dog than a wild animal. He even rolled over, legs crooking in the air, inviting a belly rub.

"That's a little intimate, don't you think?" I might have likened him to a hound, but I knew wolf behavior well—these were the kinds of actions one displayed toward one's mate.

His jaws parted, tongue lolling out, and his eyes opened, glinting with humor or something like it. With the headlights still on and providing illumination, I noticed bands of white fur near his paws. They were about an inch wide and encircled all four limbs.

"What happened there?" I asked quietly, touching one. Then I remembered the scars on his wrists that I'd seen when he'd been human. "Did you... spend time in jail?"

I imagined handcuffs, but those wouldn't have been this wide. And even if he *had* been in jail, it wasn't as if inmates spent their days in handcuffs, right?

Duncan didn't give any indication that he'd heard the question. The magic that had changed him into a wolf was starting to fade. This close, I could sense it leaving his body. I leaned back, but I continued to kneel beside him, feeling protective. It was possible the pack hadn't gone that far, and werewolves were always vulnerable when they changed.

His body morphed, fur disappearing as his wolf limbs and torso transformed into those of a man. He still lay on his back, but now I knelt beside human Duncan. *Naked* human Duncan. I got an eyeful of his anatomy before looking away.

"This is a *lot* intimate," I corrected my earlier statement.

His eyes had closed again, and he didn't respond.

I looked into the woods and vowed to watch over him until he woke.

11

"THAT WAS YOUR COUSIN, YOU SAY?" DUNCAN REFUSED TO LEAN ON me as we walked from the parking lot to the apartment complex, but he had grabbed a towel that he was pressing to his ribs. In his van, he'd found that and jeans to put on, but he apparently didn't keep a first-aid kit in there.

"Yes."

"Affable chap. Is your whole family like that? Your whole *pack*?"

After he'd woken, we'd driven the van back to the parking lot, and he'd let me talk him into going to my apartment. Like a responsible human being, or maybe just a mom, *I* had a first-aid kit.

"They weren't when I was one of them. Me leaving changed things, at least in how they interact with me." I guided him up the walkway toward my open door. The lady who'd been calling Animal Control from her balcony had disappeared. The blood spattered on the concrete reminded me of the vigor of the fight. "Are you sure you don't want me to take you to the ER?"

I felt compelled to offer, though I expected him to say no. As I well knew, there were enough oddities in werewolf blood that it raised eyebrows at hospitals. I'd given birth to my boys in the house of a doula experienced with the paranormal. I'd been afraid of being discovered as not as fully human as I looked. Fortunately, nothing had gone awry with the deliveries, and I hadn't needed more serious medical attention.

"No, thanks." Duncan eyed me sidelong, a bruise rising on his jaw, and went back to speaking about my family. "I'm fuzzy on why you left and why you choose to dull your werewolf side."

"Good. I wasn't looking to unfuzz a stranger." I tilted my head to give him an equally sidelong look. "A *strange* stranger."

"That adjective *does* apply decently to me, but we've gone into three battles together now. We can't possibly still be strangers."

"It's only been two days, and you haven't told me what you want from me. I know it's not my kindness and generous heart that has you lurking."

"You did make me espresso. That was generous. Especially since American coffee shops are outrageously expensive."

He didn't explain what he wanted from me. I didn't explain my relationship with the pack.

Instead, I helped him into my apartment and onto my couch. His sigh as he sank back into it was the only sign he gave that his wounds hurt.

"Try not to bleed on my furniture while I find my first-aid kit." I took his bloody towel from him—it had grease stains on it and couldn't possibly be hygienic—then dampened one of my own and handed it to him.

On the way through the bedroom, I eyed the dresser drawer that held the camera and the mysterious case and glanced at the two new holes in the ceiling. After my encounter with Augustus, I had more questions than answers.

Would I have learned more if I'd let him speak privately with me? Maybe, but I believed he truly would have killed me. I just didn't know why. What had changed after twenty-odd years with so little contact? And did the whole family want me dead? Or only Augustus and the two cousins he'd wrangled into helping?

As I padded back through the bedroom, first-aid kit in hand, I eyed the drawer again. It seemed an unlikely coincidence that the case and cameras, items that might have been there for years—that had *probably* been there for years—had anything to do with this. But who knew?

Though nerves twisted in my belly at the idea of returning to my childhood home, I needed to talk to my mother. I doubted *she* wanted me dead. And she might know what had crawled up Augustus's butt.

I halted in the doorway, a thought surfacing. What if Mom had died?

She was about seventy. It was possible. As I'd been considering before, maybe she had kept the others from going after me over the years, but now the restraint was gone. My shoulders slumped at the thought that she might have passed without me having a chance to say goodbye. But wouldn't someone have told me if she'd been ill?

I didn't know. Besides, werewolves tended to go out in a blaze of glory. In battle or a hunt. They didn't like to give in to the burden of time, of age and disease.

For even more reasons, I knew with certainty that I had to go home and find out what was going on.

I stepped into the living room with the first-aid kit. "I need to go after I bandage you."

Duncan perched on the edge of the couch, holding the towel to his ribs to keep the blood flow staunched. He'd also spread paper towels across the cushions, the arm rest, and on the floor under his feet.

"Go where?" He followed my gaze to the paper towels—the

rest remained on the roll on the coffee table. "I'm trying to be a conscientious guest and obey your wishes."

"That's appreciated. I need to see someone. In person." As far as I knew, my mom didn't have a phone or any other trappings of modern civilization. She lived in a cabin in the woods, with several relatives in similar homes within a few miles, and she still hunted and followed the old ways as much as she could while ignoring humanity and the outside world.

"Do you want company?" Duncan asked.

"To see my werewolf family? No. They would hate you as much as Augustus does, simply for being an outsider. Well, for being an outsider and not asking permission from them to be in their territory."

"Does that mean that if we fall in love and get married, they won't come to the wedding?" He waggled his eyebrows at me.

"They might come to stop it. Or to kill us."

"I'm getting un-fuzzier about why you left."

"It's probably not what you think." Not explaining further, I removed gauze and antiseptic and waved for him to let me see his gouges. "The pack, my family, isn't that bad when you're one of them. They're just uppity about outsiders."

"Which you are?"

"These days, yeah."

"And if you find a new potion supplier, you'll continue to be one, right? That's what you want?"

I focused on cleaning his wounds and didn't answer. I wasn't positive I knew the answer.

When the boys had lived at home, and Chad and I had been together, I'd been certain. I'd never wanted to endanger them with what I could become. But now? My plans for the future involved continuing to live in the human world, saving enough to buy a small multifamily property, living in one of the units, and being there whenever my kids came to visit. Being there when they had *grand*kids. There were aspects of the wolf way that I missed, but it was hard to imagine returning to the pack. Besides, the reason I'd left remained. My lack of ability to control myself and what I did in wolf form.

Duncan didn't clear his throat pointedly, but he did stir, his intent gaze upon me as he waited for an answer.

I didn't owe him one but caught myself saying, "It's what's safest."

A tentative knock at the door made me pause. Certain Augustus wouldn't do anything tentatively, I handed Duncan the gauze and went to answer.

Bolin stood on the threshold with two women I didn't recognize. "The plumber just left. He opened up the wall and started fixing those leaky pipes. He said the job won't take long, and then we can take care of the mold. I'll look into that. Like I said."

"There's mold here?" one of the women asked, looking at the other.

Both in their early thirties, they might have been sisters.

"Not for long," I said.

"These are potential renters who are here to look at an apartment." Bolin beamed smiles at both of them. He stood painfully straight, his face earnest, and he wasn't toting around his man purse.

I'd forgotten we had an appointment for that this evening. I'd been understandably distracted, but that didn't make me forgive myself for the lapse. Maybe having an intern around to man the leasing office, at least when my relatives were attacking me, wasn't a bad idea, after all.

"I'm allergic to mold," the other said, wrinkling her nose.

"We fix any problems as soon as our tenants alert us to them." I stepped out onto the walkway and waved into my apartment. "As you can see, I live on the premises, so if anything happens, day or night, you can let me know." Usually, I encouraged tenants to come by during office hours, but I *did* let them know I was here. Since the owners paid me a reasonable salary and let me live in one of the units, I always felt compelled to be as helpful as possible.

"I'm going to take care of the mold personally," Bolin hurried to add.

I resisted the urge to ask whether he'd found a potion that could handle that. The two ladies appeared completely human and normal. They weren't paying attention to Bolin anyway but peering past my shoulder.

When I'd gestured into the apartment, I'd meant only to indicate it was my home, but they had spotted Duncan sitting shirtless on the couch and were staring at him. I winced, certain they were also noticing that he was attempting to wrap a roll of bandage around himself. They might think the complex was attacked all the time and that this wasn't a safe area.

But the biker gang had been a fluke, and my family... hadn't been here for any of the tenants.

"Who's he?" one whispered.

Duncan looked over, smiled, and waved. "Evening, ladies."

"Oh, he's got an accent." One clasped a hand over her chest. "I *love* that accent."

Maybe they hadn't noticed the bandages and were simply ogling him. He had to be twenty years their senior.

"Does he live here? Is he a tenant?" the first asked, mold concerns forgotten.

"He lives in a van," I said more tartly than I should have. But if they rented an apartment, it should be because they liked the location, the layout, and that I maintained the complex as well as I could, not because a hunky werewolf was loitering in the area.

"Is the van *here*?" The other flipped her hair and tried to catch Duncan's eye.

"Not for long," I muttered.

Duncan didn't seem to notice the exchange. He'd turned his attention back to the bandage, and his muscles flexed nicely as he tore the end off the roll to tuck in.

"I can show you the apartment now." Bolin sounded flustered. He addressed the women but peered into my apartment, as if trying to figure out what held their attention.

"Okay," one said.

"Does it have a view of the parking lot?" the other asked, smiling. Assuming Duncan's van might be there and that he wandered shirtless in and out of it all day?

"There's some grass and trees to look at between the unit and the parking lot," Bolin said, "but you'd be able to see your car from the living room if that's what you're wondering."

"Not exactly."

They giggled as they followed him away.

"Thanks for showing them the unit," I called after Bolin.

He waved a hand in acknowledgment.

"Do I get a bonus if I flirt with prospective tenants and convince them to sign a lease?" Duncan asked after I closed the door and returned to the couch.

I'd thought he'd been oblivious to their interest but apparently not. My first instinct was to squash his ego, but he'd been too helpful today for me to want to snark at him.

"We don't have a budget for bonuses for itinerant werewolves, but if those two sign a lease, I'll let you metal detect on the grounds."

"Oh, enticing. That could prove fruitful. And would my van be able to stay in a guest or staff parking spot without fear of being towed?"

"It hasn't been towed yet, has it?"

"It has not. It's possible my charisma is keeping you from following through on your threats."

"I've also been busy." I would have to thank Bolin for manning the office and giving the tour. "And I need to continue to be busy. In the woods north of Monroe." I eyed the night sky outside the window. It wasn't that late, but it got dark early this time of year, making it *feel* late. Visiting werewolves, even one's own mother, at night wasn't the best idea, but it was easier to slip away outside of the complex's office hours. "Before I head out, do you need a ride to a healer of the paranormal or anything like that?"

"That won't be necessary. I have an excellent immune system, nearly as vigorous and virile as the rest of me, so I heal quickly. I'll remain here snuggled up to your first-aid kit. I do have a few other fang punctures to attend." Duncan waved to his jeans and whatever gouges lay under the denim.

"Attend away, but do it in your van." I grabbed the kit, pointed to the door, and offered him a hand up.

"You're kicking me out? I was very careful not to bleed on your furniture." Duncan looked at the crinkled paper towels blanketing the couch, then licked his thumb and rubbed what might have been blood off the edge of the coffee table.

I made a note to sanitize the furniture later. "I'm going to lock up my apartment while I'm gone."

He was too interested in the wolf case for me to leave it where he could find it. Maybe I would even put it in the glove compartment of my truck and take it with me. Of course, bringing a magical item into werewolf territory might not be a good idea either. The pack would be able to sense its magic, and if it turned out that Mom was gone and my cousins were all gunning for me...

"I can lock your door on my way out," Duncan offered, his eyebrows up, his face the picture of innocence.

I didn't trust that look—or him—and gripped his elbow to help him to the door—or maybe hoist him *out* the door. "You can't lock a deadbolt on the way out, and this neighborhood isn't as safe as it used to be."

He opened his mouth as if he might protest further—which

made me doubly suspicious about why he wanted to hang out here while I was gone.

"Besides," I added, "you're heading off with that list of ingredients to find me an alchemist who can make my potion, right?"

"You think I should do that when I've so recently been grievously injured?" He waved at his bandaged chest.

"After you spoke of the excessively virile vigor of your immune system? Yes, that should be easy." I handed him the first-aid kit in case he needed to bandage anything else.

"Very well, my lady. I shall depart. Can I at least have some more of your fine chocolate to take with me? I haven't eaten in some time."

I was tempted to say *no*, but he was doing me a favor. If he found a new alchemist to supply me with potions, I would buy him a whole stack of chocolate bars.

As I moved into the kitchen to snap off a couple more squares for him, I caught him gazing thoughtfully at my bedroom. Despite his proclamations of my beauty, I doubted his musings involved us naked together.

No, I decided. I wouldn't leave the magical case in my apartment.

12

My truck carried me off Highway 2 in Monroe, through the town, and to the north, where I headed down roads that I hadn't driven in ages. The magical case wasn't in my glove compartment. On the way out of the complex, I'd run into Bolin, who'd been leaving for the day, promising the prospective tenants had liked what they'd seen and would be back after they scrounged up money for the deposit. On a whim, hopefully not an *unwise* whim, I'd given him the case and asked him to either research it or ask his father what it was.

Bolin's eyes hadn't lit up with covetous interest when he'd regarded it. Instead, he'd called it a nice wolf box, then informed me that the word box came from the Greek *pyxis*, which meant a container made from boxwood, or maybe the Latin *buxus,* which had the same meaning as *pyxis.*

Maybe it was strange that I trusted my new intern more than Duncan, but I'd gotten a feel for the kind of person Bolin was on Day 1. My read on Duncan was sketchy. *He* was sketchy.

A lot of houses had been built along the back roads since the last time I'd been through Monroe, but once I drove out into unincorporated territory and the pavement turned to gravel and pot-hole-filled dirt, the homes grew infrequent. Around town, there was a lot of farmland, but out here, forests and wetlands dominated, with trees growing close to the roads, evergreen branches blocking most of the night sky. Now and then, a dog barked at a fence, and houselights filtered through the woods, but I trusted my mother still didn't have many neighbors.

She didn't live in the home I'd grown up in. That had burned in a fire, possibly an arson, back when a rival pack, the Cascade Crushers, had competed for this territory. Since first arriving from the Old World generations before, our packs had feuded with each other, like the Hatfields and McCoys. Our territorial kind could start battles that lasted generations—until one pack was destroyed or driven out. Peace treaties were rare, though Raoul and I had once spoken of bringing our packs together. That hadn't been meant to be.

By the time I'd left, the Crushers had departed for Canada, saying they longed for land where fewer humans intruded upon the forests and game was more plentiful. That might have been true, but they might also have been devastated by the loss of Raoul. They'd never come to me to speak of it, and I'd been too ashamed and scared to go to them.

A breeze pushed the clouds across the sky, and the nearly full moon peeked out, casting shadows between the trees and bathing the side of my face in its silvery light. It made my skin waken, as if the moon could convey the warmth of sunlight. For a werewolf, it almost did, though it was *magic* that one felt, not the sun's radiation.

My blood tingled in my veins, and an aliveness that I hadn't felt in a long time crept into me. As I had long ago, I had the urge to change forms and run through the forest, to feel the autumn breeze caressing my face as I sought prey to hunt.

I swallowed, gripped the steering wheel tightly, and attempted to sublimate that urge. I was coming out to get my questions answered, not to hunt, and definitely not to change into a wolf. If I needed meat, I could delve into the salmon-and-sausage gift box I'd picked up on the way out of town. At the last minute, I'd decided I should bring an offering that a carnivore would appreciate.

Ahead, my high beams played over a wooden address sign nailed to a tree. Above the house numbers, a wolf howled at the moon. It reminded me of the case, though the wolf on that was showing its pointed teeth rather than howling.

I turned up the winding dirt driveway, trees hemming it in on either side. As my headlights swung with the truck's movement, they briefly highlighted two eyes in the distance. They disappeared from view almost as soon as I saw them, but nerves made my heart thump in my chest. The eyes hadn't been *glowing*, like those of the minions that had attacked me, but they might have belonged to a werewolf.

"Not that unusual," I told myself.

Most of the younger generation of werewolves from our pack lived in the suburbs and were at least somewhat incorporated into human life, but they came out to visit and hunt. I suspected most of the family would be here for the full moon. Maybe some already were. My senses, feeling more alive out here, told me that more than one wolf lurked in the woods.

Mom's two-room log cabin came into view, surrounded by evergreens that towered high, not allowing enough sunlight to filter down for a lawn. Mossy rocks framed the cleared gravel driveway near the front door, and fir and pine needles scattered the packed earth around the home's stone foundation. A river rock chimney rose from the ground on one end of the cabin, and smoke wafted out of it. A dented Jeep Wrangler was parked in the driveway, a vehicle I didn't recognize, but it looked like something Mom would own.

It was hard not to feel like a complete stranger as I drove closer. No, not a stranger. An *intruder*. Normally, I would have called someone before visiting, but Mom didn't have a phone, and there wasn't cell reception out here anyway.

Before I reached the parking area, two huge gray wolves loped out of the trees. Big males, they each looked powerful enough to take down a buck by themselves—or rip the fender off my truck.

Since I was driving slowly, I didn't have to slam on the brakes, but their appearance startled me. Were these more cousins? They seemed vaguely familiar, but after so many years, my memories had grown fuzzy. One was young, maybe young enough that I hadn't met him before.

They stood in the driveway, facing me with their hackles up. They blocked the way.

Sweat dampened my palms where I gripped the wheel. I might have veered off, weaved through trees, and reached the cabin, but I trusted they would continue to impede me if I tried that.

"Guess I'm parking here." I rolled down the window. "Either of you boys need a ride?" I pointed to an Uber sticker on my windshield.

Before all this craziness had started, I'd driven for the ride-sharing outfit a couple of evenings a week, earning extra on the side in an attempt to reach my financial goals. My truck was on the verge of falling out of their minimum requirements, but it could have carried numerous werewolves in the bed without trouble.

Neither pack member moved out of the road, tempted by my offer. The older wolf, a touch of white at his muzzle, curled his lips to show me his fangs. The younger gazed intently through the windshield. With curiosity? It was hard to tell. His nostrils twitched as he tested the air, maybe trying to figure out who I was. Or... *what* I was? This close to needing another dose of the potion, I probably didn't smell that different from a normal werewolf, but I didn't know that for certain.

After turning off the truck, I grabbed the gift box and slid out. The brisk night air chilled me through my hoodie, and a touch of frost already edged the roots of trees. With the engine off, I had no trouble hearing the soft growls coming from the older wolf. The other cocked his head and looked at the box.

"I came to see my mother." I pointed toward the cabin, a lamp glowing yellow behind one of the windows. "I'm her daughter, Luna."

Both wolves changed, magic blurring the air around them, obscuring the details of the transformation. Soon, two men with powerful builds crouched in the driveway, naked.

The older man, with gray shot through his beard and a bald—or shaven—head, was familiar, though he'd had hair the last time I'd seen him. Marco was another cousin, Augustus's older brother. Had he heard about Duncan and the fight yet? Or... I squinted at him. Had he *been* at the fight? One of the wolves in the woods?

"We *know* who you are," Marco said, his deep voice as much a snarl now as it had been as a wolf. "*Traitor.*"

I opened my mouth, wanting to protest that leaving home hadn't been a betrayal to the family. I might have betrayed *Raoul's* family... but they were long gone. My memory was fuzzy after all these years, but they hadn't seemed to blame me for that night, for his end. Strange that my own family held more of a grudge.

"*I* didn't know," the younger wolf said. "I've only heard about Aunt Umbra's daughter."

"That's because you're a baby, Emilio," Marco said.

"I'm twenty-three."

"A baby. And a runt at that. You're lucky Tony doesn't floss his teeth with you."

"I've seen the gristle hanging from between his teeth. Tony doesn't floss ever." The younger man—Emilio—sniffed the air, as interested in the gift box now as he had been before. With a broad face and big ears, he reminded me more of a Labrador than a wolf.

Marco sniffed the air—no, he was sniffing *me*. "You smell so human, Luna."

"Yeah, I get that all the time."

He squinted at me. "You're not welcome here. Not since you *altered* yourself to mate with a human and have puny human offspring."

More than being insulted on my children's behalf, and my life choices, it bothered me that my cousins knew that much about what I'd been up to the last twenty-plus years. They hadn't visited or called, so I'd assumed they'd mostly forgotten about me. But Augustus had mentioned my mother and aunt keeping tabs on me. Maybe it had all been innocuous, but I couldn't help but think of the hidden cameras.

"The last I heard, this is my mother's house, not yours," I said. "*She* can tell me if I'm not welcome."

Which she might very well do. I looked toward the cabin. Other than the light, there wasn't much sign of life. That might be Marco's Jeep, not Mom's.

"I'm sure she will," Marco said. "You disappointed her. You disappointed *everyone*."

"It was more than two decades ago. What I chose to do with my life shouldn't have affected you then, and I don't know why you're worrying about it now."

"Because you are *here* in our forest with your altered *human-ness*. And you didn't have the offspring you *should* have had, werewolf pups. You were supposed to mate with an alpha to make strong offspring. The pack is *dying*, Luna. All werewolves are. We're losing our magic. You knew that even then, and you left anyway."

"I had to after... After." Memories whispered through my mind, of a moonlit autumn night not so different from this one, of frost crunching in the leaves under our paws as Raoul and I ran through the forest. Before our tempers had flared, we'd been on the hunt of an injured stag, our blood singing with all that it meant to be a wolf.

"His death didn't change anything. More, it proved you were the alpha female, that you could have had any male—any *were-wolf* male—you wished and produced strong offspring to carry on our lineage, our destiny. Instead, you sterilized yourself." Scathing, Marco sneered as he looked me up and down.

Tired of the conversation, I waved a dismissive hand at him and headed toward the front door. If my mother wasn't here, there was no reason for me to stand and endure this.

Marco moved to block me. "You shouldn't bother her with whatever trivial crap brought you here."

He was as big and strong as Augustus, and fear and uncertainty jolted me. But I kept walking, knowing he would be more of a bully if I showed him that fear. Feelings of anger and belligerence trickled through my veins as well, ancient instincts stirring with the desire to call the wolf out and challenge him to a fight. Once, I'd been a match for any of my cousins. Once, only an alpha male had been strong enough to defeat me.

But that wasn't the case anymore. I had to be careful. I had to tamp down the wolf. Even if the potion's effectiveness had waned enough for my lupine side to rise, I was older now. With startling certainty, I realized my muzzle would also be gray in wolf form.

Emilio pointed at the gift box. "That doesn't look trivial. Aunt Umbra might want that. She should have any gifts that people bring, especially now."

That comment made me pause, unease replacing my anger and fear. Was something wrong with Mom?

"Aunt Umbra should eat quality meat and organs." Marco lifted a hand, as if he might knock the box to the ground. "Not salted and pulverized human garbage squeezed into log shapes."

"Are you sure?" Emilio grabbed Marco's arm to stop the blow, and he stepped closer to me—to the gift. "It smells good. Do my nostrils detect smoked salmon?"

Marco opened his mouth to further demonstrate his surliness, but light slashed into the night from the cabin. The front door had opened.

Mom stood on the threshold, tall and lean in a flannel shirt and hiking trousers. Her face was chiseled, her brown eyes intent, her long white hair pulled back into a braid. She looked as straight and proud as I remembered, but deep creases lined her face, and it lacked the color, the healthy vigor, of the past. Her once olive skin seemed as pale as the hair that had been lush and black when I'd left home.

"Return to your hunt, boys," she said. "I'll talk to my daughter."

13

"Come, Luna." Despite her paleness, Mom's voice remained strong and authoritative, and she radiated magical power. Her eyes even seemed to gleam as they reflected the moonlight.

I opened the gift box and withdrew a salami log, handing it to Emilio as I passed. So far, he was the only male family member I'd encountered this week who didn't hate me. At least not yet. I didn't know how much of my story he was familiar with.

His eyebrows rose in surprise, but he grinned fiercely as he clutched the salami to his chest.

"Disgusting," Marco said, but he stepped back. He nodded to my mother and made no further move to intercept me.

Emilio sniffed the end of the salami and grinned wider. "*Delicious.*"

Marco shook his head again.

"Maybe Aurora was right." Emilio nodded to me. "Maybe you're all right."

I recognized the name of one of my nieces, but she and her sister Jasmine had been toddlers when last I'd seen them. I wasn't sure how Aurora could have vouched for me. Still, I would be happy to learn that the *entire* family didn't hate me.

Salami in hand, Emilio trotted off into the woods. He sent suspicious glances over his shoulder at Marco as he went, as if believing the older man would come after him and steal away the snack.

"Emilio is your cousin Leopold's youngest." My mother watched as I climbed up to the cabin's front porch, her eyes hard to read.

Was she pleased to see me? Or had she never wanted to see me again? When I'd left, she hadn't understood my strong emotions, my unwillingness to accept that losing oneself to one's werewolf instincts was perfectly normal, but she hadn't been angry with me. That, however, had been before I found those potions.

"He seems like a decent guy." I didn't remark on Marco—or Augustus.

"He's a puppy, but that's what happens with the runts."

I didn't point out that Emilio had clearly grown out of that runtiness. He'd been big both as a man and a wolf.

Mom stepped back, lifting an arm to invite me into the cabin.

That was something, at least. She glanced at the opened gift box, a few summer sausages and packets of smoked salmon remaining.

Knowing werewolves as I did, I'd opted for the meat-and-fish-lovers package, no pesky sweets or cheeses contaminating the offerings. I did, however, lay two bars of dark chocolate, each spruced up with sea salt and honey-bourbon bacon, next to the box when I set it on her table. After all, Mom had been the one who'd once introduced me to chocolate. Milk was far too anemic and sweet, she'd assured me, but a wolf's palette could be tempted by the bolder and richer flavors of a good dark.

"You wouldn't know since *you* weren't a runt," she added, glancing outside before closing the door firmly.

Marco remained in the driveway, as if he suspected I might try to assassinate my mother, and he needed to stand by as her body-guard. If he cared about his aunt, then I could respect him for that, even if he was being an ass to me.

"No," I agreed.

Runt-ness hadn't been my problem.

"You look like you've kept yourself reasonably fit." Mom looked me up and down. "If diminished. Your magic is barely noticeable."

"I know. I'm sure you know why."

The whole pack seemed to know far more about me than I would have wished.

She tilted her head as she regarded me. "I don't exactly. You never came back and explained. I originally heard from your half-brother in Lake Forest Park that you'd married a human and were having children."

"Yeah. It—deciding to take an alchemical potion that subli-mates my werewolf urges—was because of Raoul."

"I know your grief after his passing was why you left, but..."

"He didn't pass, Mother. I lost my temper and *killed* him."

The blunt words stirred the old memories again. A hunt gone poorly that had led to a heated argument that had turned into a fight under the moon, our jaws snapping, our muscles surging, our fangs sinking through fur and into vulnerable flesh. After all these years, the memory of that night remained sharp, though it some-times felt as if it had been a dream—a nightmare. If Raoul had been an enemy, it wouldn't have been so bad, but we'd been lovers, passionate youths who hadn't cared that we were from rival packs. We'd always thought we would find a way to be together, that we would become mates and hunt side-by-side forever.

"Thus causing him to pass." Mom shrugged indifferently, as if that moment hadn't destroyed me and altered the course of my entire life. "If he couldn't fend you off when your temper was raised, he didn't deserve to be an alpha and pack leader. Another would have killed him, if not you."

"He *did* deserve it, and he... could have fended me off if he'd truly wanted it, if he'd been willing to kill me."

"You underestimate the power you had then. Even if he loved you, his survival instincts would have kicked in. If he'd been able to best you, he would have."

I shook my head. She hadn't known Raoul, not the way I had. He'd been strong, fit, and in line to lead the Crushers one day, but he'd also been a lover and a poet. In his human form, he'd composed music and written lyrics. Unlike me, he'd never lost his sanity in his wolf form, never let his wild instincts get the best of him.

"He did love me," I said quietly, looking out a back window toward the dark woods. "That's why it was such a betrayal that I let myself attack him."

"It was the battle lust." Mom shrugged again. "We all have it. He shouldn't have roused your temper during a hunt. We are not humans, my daughter. I see now, as I saw then, that you believed you were in the wrong, but you were guided by your wolf instincts. To establish dominance or keep the peace in the pack, alpha males and females may turn on threats, even mates, at any time. Our blood guides us to show our strength, to make sure the pack knows not to threaten us. I drove your half-siblings' father out when he didn't continue to be suitable."

Sometimes, I wondered if that was what happened to *my* father too, but I couldn't remember him at all. She'd told me before that he had been a lone wolf passing through, an intriguing one-night stand. Whether that was the truth or not, I didn't know.

"We must keep those who make the pack strong," Mom continued, "not those who are liabilities. That is the way of the wolf."

"We live as humans *most* of the time, Mother. In the world of humans, it's a crime to kill another person, a crime punishable by death."

She made a disgusted noise and chopped the air with her arm. "Being forced to live in their world does not mean we can be bound by their culture and laws. We have our own ways. And their world is killing us, their ever-expanding population encroaching on nature and destroying the Earth's magic. *Our* magic. We can't even become the bipedfuris—the in-between form—and add new blood to the pack anymore. It's been centuries since I've heard of one of us succeeding in that and in using a bite to turn a man or woman, to bring a new werewolf into a pack. When you left to mate with a human and have *human* children... Luna, those boys should have been werewolves. The world doesn't *need* any more humans. That you didn't mate with your own kind, especially when you were so powerful..."

I didn't argue because I understood her disappointment. I couldn't regret the birth of my sons, nor could I imagine having stayed with the pack, but I knew why she was upset.

"I always hoped if I gave you time and space, you would one day return, that the call of the moon would bring you back. I didn't expect..." Her eyes bored into my back as I continued to look out the window. "These potions... What *exactly* have you done to yourself? Your magic doesn't seem quite as dead as Augustus said, but I can sense, as I said, you are diminished."

I made myself turn and face her. "Like I said, the potion sublimates the wolf and the urge to turn."

"Yes, but are the effects permanent?"

"No, I have to take it every month, ideally before the full moon. I'm..." I glanced toward the woods again, the silver light filtering through the branches. "I'm due."

"So it's not irrevocable." Hope flickered in her eyes. "If you stopped consuming it, you could return to us."

"That's technically true."

"Then you must. The pack, the forest, the *hunt* is your destiny."

I shook my head. I'd chosen my destiny years ago. Of course, with the boys gone—the boys *grown*—there was less binding me to my current path, but I would hate to die in a hunt or a fight for dominance with another werewolf—Augustus's face flashed in my mind—and have Austin and Cameron lose me. Just because they'd started new lives didn't mean they would never need advice from their mother again.

"Are you still fertile?" Mom asked, the blunt question startling me.

"Er, I'm forty-five."

She gazed at me, waiting. Did that not answer her question?

"Technically, I guess, but women don't usually have kids at my age. I'm not sure I could conceive if I wanted to." And I did not want to. I didn't even want to have a husband again—a *mate*, as the pack called it. Not after the hurt and betrayal of Chad sleeping around and stealing from us.

"*Human* women," Mom said. "Our kind, as long as we eat our traditional diets and bask in the magic of the moon each month, sometimes have longer periods of fertility."

"I'm not basking in anything, Mother."

"And that is greatly problematic. As it was when you became mates with that... strange human man. What did you even see in him?"

Yes, it seemed she had indeed been keeping an eye on me, if from a distance. I'd never introduced Chad to her or anyone else in my werewolf family.

"In the beginning, he was handsome and dashing and really into me." Actually, as I'd learned later, Chad had been really *into* werewolves. When we'd been dating, he'd figured out what I was, and he'd always hoped he would see me change. A few times, he'd hidden my potions and tried to make that happen. That had been the beginning of the end for us, the start of my wariness toward him.

"So mundane. So human."

"He is that. Why did you need me to have werewolf children? My half-siblings mated and had—"

"They never had as much power as you, as much *magic*. Their offspring are fine, and they contribute to our well-being, but they are not suitable heirs to the *power* of the pack. You would have been. You still *could* be."

"The power of the pack?"

She'd spoken often of *the way of the wolf* to describe our people's cultural traditions, but I hadn't heard her use this other phrase before.

"Our legacy." Mom looked toward the cabin's other room, the door open, but only a nightstand and the bed, furs and hides draping the mattress, were visible. "When you were born, I had such joy and hope. You were the most promising of your generation. Of *several* generations. I thought you might be able to do what I never could, what my siblings couldn't either. Find a way to bring back the magic of the werewolf bite, the ability to become the bipedfuris and change worthy humans into our kind. We *must* find that magic again." She spread her arms. "We are dying, Luna. Our gene pool is so limited these days that we must breed with our relatives. It is not ideal."

"No." I thought of Duncan, last seen bandaging his wounds, and almost pointed out that it didn't help that the pack drove out any werewolves that visited from other areas, but that wouldn't have made much of a difference. Even when one included the Old World—Europe—and the Wild Worlds—other continents—there weren't that many werewolves left on Earth.

"If you could come back to us," she said, "and you could accept your destiny, you would be my heir. You could receive... all that I have, all that I have been entrusted with."

"I don't want your stuff, Mom." I waved to indicate the cabin and its contents.

"I speak of more than *stuff*." She frowned sternly at me.

I almost missed her expression because a shadow moved outside the window, making me jump. A wolf loped away into the woods.

Had that been Marco? Passing by on his way to hunt? Or had he been listening at the window? It wasn't open, but a wolf's ears were keen. It wouldn't have mattered.

Mom must not have noticed because she walked into the bedroom, opened a drawer, and withdrew a black-velvet-covered box. It was four times the size of a typical jewelry box, at least for a ring or earrings, but it reminded me of one.

"There are many who want this," she said quietly, glancing toward the window. Maybe she *had* seen the wolf run past. "But in our pack, it has traditionally been passed down from mother to daughter. There was once another artifact that passed from alpha male to son—or whoever became the alpha after him—but that has been lost. Some believe that is when the power of the bite was lost, but that may only be myth. It is not only *our* pack, with our magical artifacts, that have lost that magic. It's believed that no werewolves left in the world today retain that ability."

I didn't know what to say—nobody had ever spoken to me of artifacts or a destiny when I'd been young—so I waited quietly. Mom closed her eyes, rumbling a soft growl before she opened the lid of the box.

A gold medallion on a thick gold chain lay mounted within. A wolf in profile was engraved on the front, its jaws open, its fangs sharp. It wasn't the *exact* wolf on the case that Duncan's magic detector had found, but the similarity struck me. There had to be a link.

Mom touched a finger to the medallion, and it glowed silver, its illumination similar to that coming from the moon outside.

Even from a couple of feet away, I could sense magic emanating from it, power tingling in the air.

She lowered her hand and gazed intently at me. "Touch the medallion."

"I won't get zapped and knocked across the room, will I?"

"That only happens to enemies of the pack who are trying to steal it."

That wasn't the most reassuring answer. What if, because I took the potion, the medallion considered *me* an enemy? My cousins sure did these days.

"Touch it," Mom repeated in a no-nonsense tone.

Since disobeying one's mother was always a bad idea, especially one's *werewolf* mother, I braced myself and lifted a finger. When I touched the tip to the cool gold, it didn't knock me across the room. Its magic seemed welcoming rather than hostile, almost inviting me to lift the chain and put on the medallion. It even glowed faintly, though not as much as it had at Mom's touch.

"I *knew* it." Her eyes gleamed in triumph. "At least, I hoped this would be the case. Others in the family thought it wouldn't respond to you, but I believed it would. If you stop taking that odious alchemical concoction, I believe it would respond to you as much as it does to me." She lifted her chin. "It does *not* respond to Bianca. Augustus's mate."

The significance of that wasn't clear to me. "Did you have everyone in the pack touch it or something? Like a test?"

"Recently, I had a meeting and brought some of the pack in to tell them about the medallion and to see if it reacted to anyone's touch. Female werewolves who might be acceptable... backups if you didn't come back."

I lowered my hand. "I'm not coming back."

"You must." Mom closed the lid. "You are the pack's hope, and to be connected with your own kind is the way of the wolf." Her gaze drifted to the kitchen, and she walked to a cabinet, opening it, then stepping aside so I could see inside. Containers of prescription drugs were lined up in front of a stack of bowls.

Uncertainty and dread crept into me. "Why did you feel compelled to have that meeting?"

"I have been ill. According to the human doctors that the pack's wise wolf urged me to see, I have cancer. I'm dying."

I slumped against the table. I'd been afraid of that.

"The wise wolf didn't have that term for my disease but agrees that age has crept up on me and that my aura is fading. I seek to set my affairs in order and do whatever I can to ensure the legacy of our line, the continuation of the pack."

Words wouldn't come as I stared at her in distress. After so long, I shouldn't have been shocked that she had grown older, and of course I'd known she would eventually die. But she'd always been so strong that I struggled to imagine her succumbing to a disease that afflicted mundane human beings.

"I won't take their treatments, their medications." She flicked a finger toward the cupboard. The row of pills did look largely decorative, like she might have briefly mused over taking them when she'd first removed them from the bag, then decided against it. "That is not the way of nature, of the wolf."

"If you did receive treatment, would be it be possible to overcome the cancer and live longer?" I didn't know if I should respect her wishes or try to urge her to reconsider the doctor's advice. If she had something treatable, she ought to do that. What if it was only stubborn distaste for all things human that led her to shun the medicine?

"I need you to stop taking that concoction and return to the pack," Mom said without answering my question.

"I... I'm very sorry that you're ill, Mother. But I don't think the pack wants me to return." My cousin's words echoed in my mind: *You smell so human.* "Did you know... do you know *why* Augustus is trying to kill me?"

"Is he? I didn't think any of the pack were having contact with you."

"They weren't. Until yesterday. Something changed." I thought of the cameras and the magical case, but we'd found those *after* Augustus had first called.

Of course, Duncan had shown up about then. He was up to something, but did it have anything to do with my pack? He was an outsider, and Augustus hadn't seemed to recognize him.

"I am not sure what has changed for him," Mom said, "unless my telling the pack about my condition prompted his actions. I don't know why it would, however. And that was over a month ago. When did Augustus visit you?"

Visit. As if we'd chatted over tea and macarons.

"Just yesterday," I said.

Was that right? It seemed like weeks' worth of events had passed in the last two days.

"Perhaps, if you come on a hunt with the pack, you could get some answers." Mom looked toward the window. "The moon is almost full. When it is, the pack will hunt together, as it always does. Emotions will be high, inhibitions lowered, as is always the case when we are in our true form."

As I well remembered. Still haunted by Raoul's death, I shuddered.

"Truths might be revealed," Mom said, watching me.

"I..."

"Don't take the concoction again. Let yourself remember what it's like to be a wolf, to be *yourself*. And perhaps you will find what you seek."

"I... I'll think about it."

"Good," she said softly, closing the medallion box and holding it to her chest. "Good."

14

RAIN FELL THE NEXT MORNING, PUDDLES FORMING IN THE PARKING lot of the apartment complex. I stood under the overhang of the balcony above the leasing office and sipped my coffee, attempting to get myself in the mindset for work. Earlier, after helping a tenant who'd locked herself out, I'd taken a walk around the grounds. Duncan's van wasn't in the lot.

For days, I'd been trying to get rid of him, and I especially hadn't wanted him lurking around, finding a way to snoop in my apartment while I'd been gone. But now... Now, a strange loneliness filled me. No, it was more than that. Since the boys had left, I'd grown used to loneliness. I read and turned on the television for company at night, and that was usually enough. Uncertainty and unease were what I felt now. I was being stalked by mortality. My mother's, for certain, and it was also possible that Augustus would show up again and finish what he'd started. If Duncan wasn't here to help fend him off, could I survive my cousin's assault?

Maybe if I allowed the wolf to return. In my youth, I'd been a match for anyone in the pack, even the strong males. But what would it be like now that I'd grown older? If I turned, would my knee ache, as it often did in my human form? Would I be feeble and weak? Would I have forgotten everything my instincts had once known? How to hunt and kill my prey? How to fight off dangerous rivals?

It occurred to me that I'd now spent more years of my life sublimating the wolf and being a full human than I had in my normal state. What if those tingles of magic were only teasing me and it turned out that I *couldn't* turn anymore?

I wished I had someone to talk to about all this. If Duncan returned, maybe I would share some of these feelings with him. He wasn't anyone I could trust, but I *wished* he were. Until this week, I hadn't realized that I missed having a partner and a confidant. It had been so long since my husband had been that. And my sons... They knew nothing of my heritage, my magic. I'd always sheltered them, trying so hard to be a normal human being for them and their teachers and friends. Anyone who might judge them for having a weird mom.

Bolin's gleaming G-wagon entered the parking lot, sending up spray as the tires rolled through puddles.

I was in enough of a funk that talking to my unwanted intern actually sounded appealing. But I couldn't help but look wistfully toward the street, hoping Duncan would show up, whether I should want that or not.

"I did offer to let him metal detect the grounds," I murmured.

Would that draw him? Maybe not. It was possible something interesting was buried in the greenbelt over there, but I had a feeling his metal detecting had been a pretext for something. A way to spy on me?

It was hard to imagine being someone interesting enough for anyone to want to spy on, but all I had to do was think of the hidden cameras to be reminded that *someone* had been keeping an eye on me. And Duncan was definitely interested in the magical case.

"Hey, Luna." Bolin half-grunted the greeting.

With bags under his eyes, he approached, carrying two large coffee cups. Judging by the caramel drizzled over the whipped cream of one, he meant to drink his daily quota of calories. Possibly before nine.

"Hi. Is one of those for me?" I had my own coffee, thanks to my home espresso maker, so I didn't need a drink, but I rarely saw someone carrying two for himself. Maybe he'd talked one of those girls who'd been touring an apartment into a morning coffee date.

"Uhm. No." Bolin stopped a few steps away and curled the cups protectively—or maybe that was *possessively*—to his chest. "Since the workday here starts at an ungodly hour, I knew I'd need extra fortification to make it through the morning."

"It's 7:57."

He looked blankly at me.

"Didn't you have to take any morning classes in college? Get up early for spelling-bee practice?"

"Not my senior year. I picked late-start stuff. And you always want to study for bees when your brain is sharpest."

"Which is not at eight a.m. for you?"

"I get in my groove around one."

"P.M.?"

"No."

"Ah."

Bolin squinted assessingly at me but must have decided I was unlikely to jump him for his coffee. Either of them. He stepped under the overhang with me, then lowered his voice to a conspiratorial whisper. "I have news."

"If it's that Jonas in A-4 splices cable from his neighbor and doesn't pay, I've already given him a warning. I told him he's not getting a new garbage disposal until he starts giving Linda next-door money for what he's been sneakily sharing with her."

"Er, I haven't examined the cable lines of the tenants." Bolin yawned and wiped his tired eyes with the back of one hand, not spilling a drop of the coffee. "Do I *need* to do that?"

"It's good to know what's going on."

"I think I'd have to live here to learn as much about the goings-on as you." His nose wrinkled with distaste as he looked around the grounds. The well-manicured and assiduously tended grounds. Only someone who lived a luxury lifestyle could have sneered at them.

"There are some vacant units if you want to move in. On a clear day, E-33 has a view of the dumpsters."

His nose wrinkled even more. "I can't believe I came in extra early to help you."

"It's three minutes before eight." I glanced at the time on my phone and waved at the office hours posted outside the door. "Now, *two* minutes before eight."

"I can't believe I came in *slightly* early to help you."

"Tell me what help you're offering so I know how appreciative to be of your sacrifice."

Bolin lowered his voice again—further. "It's about the case."

I perked up at that. I hadn't forgotten about it, but the previous night's events, especially Mom's revelation that she was dying, had distracted me. "Did you research it?"

"Yeah, and I asked my father about it. He was really into it, like it was a piece of fine art or something. He got a magnifying glass out and could tell it was druid craftsmanship and magic. Old World kind. He said artifacts like that are really rare, especially in our country. They hardly ever make it out of Europe."

I thought of the medallion Mom had shown me and wondered what a druid would think of it.

"Even over there," Bolin continued, "real druids are scarce

these days. Magic has been bleeding out of the world for genera-tions, at least according to my dad. But your case is probably really old and was made when there were more crafters around, more people with the gift. He figured it's centuries old, at least."

"Interesting."

And puzzling. It wouldn't have been entirely mystifying if one of my family members had hidden something to do with were-wolves at my place—maybe trying to hide it from the rest of the pack?—but I hadn't crossed paths with many druids. If the case had been made with their magic, it might not have anything to do with my mom's medallion after all. Werewolves had their own magic, their own crafters, though they were also scarce these days.

"There's some writing on the bottom too," Bolin added. "It's faded and hard to read, so I didn't notice it at first. I left Dad painstakingly copying it. He said he'll get out some books and see if he can translate it."

"Did he figure out how to open the case and see what's inside?"

"I don't think so. He said it would be wise to research it thor-oughly before attempting to do so because it's ensorcelled."

"Yeah." I rubbed the hand that had been zapped, glad I hadn't tried to force the lid open.

"*I* might have tried to open it," Bolin admitted.

"How'd that go?"

"This is an iced mocha because my father suggested a cold pack for my hand." Bolin held up the drink with the caramel sauce drizzled over the whipped cream, and I glimpsed a bandage on his palm.

"Is it numbing you suitably?"

"Yup." He slurped from the straw. "We took some pictures and made notes. When do you need me to bring the case back?"

I considered Duncan's interest. As far as I knew, that hadn't changed. I didn't know him well enough to guess whether he would break into a locked apartment to steal something. From what I'd seen of his career, thus far, the magic- and metal-detector adventures weren't illegal, but... who knew how far his endeavors for finding lost things went? What if those lost things were stashed in someone's sock drawer? And was it strange that I missed Duncan's company *and* was debating if he was a thief?

"Why don't you keep it for a couple of days?" I suggested. "While you guys study it."

"Are you sure? My father said it's really valuable, at least to those who know what it is." Bolin sipped from one of his cups. "He's got a safe he can keep it in, I guess. You wouldn't want it just lying around. If someone who doesn't know anything about magic and artifacts gets their hands on it, it could end up at a flea market."

"I'd think the good-looking wolf carved into the front would make someone think it has more value than a five-dollar tchotchke."

"Okay, it might end up on Etsy. Do you know the origins of that word?"

"Tchotchke? It's Yiddish, isn't it?"

"Originally, it comes from the Polish word for trinket. It was adopted into Yiddish slang as *tshatshke* and popular with Jewish Americans last century." A nose wrinkle suggested Bolin might not think it was still popular and that I was an old fart for using it.

"Did you ever have to spell either at a bee?" I asked.

"No, but they'd be easy."

"If you say so." I'd only typed the word a few times, and Auto-Correct had had a heyday with my attempts.

After another contemplative sip, Bolin said, "The wolf element on the case is what's most interesting to me. It's not an *atypical* druid symbol, but it's not that common of one either."

"Do you think there's any tie to *werewolves*? Did they ever interact much with druids?" It was hard for me to dismiss the idea that Mom's medallion and that box were somehow linked.

"Werewolves?" Bolin mouthed.

"Yeah, from the Old English werwulf, which means *wer,* the old-school word for man, and wolf." I gave him an arch look, wondering if he would be surprised that I knew that. Werewolves, of course, were more pertinent to me than tchotchkes, so I'd had occasion to read about them.

"I *know* about the word origins—including the French *loup-garou,* the Greek *lycanthrope,* and the Russian *vulkodlak,* among others—but werewolves don't exist. They're fictional beings from fairy tales. Not like druids."

"You don't think so, huh?" I was surprised that he couldn't sense the magic in me, or at least in Duncan, whom he'd been close to now. After all, I could sense that Bolin had a smidgen of the paranormal about him. "There are words for them in a lot of languages."

"Many classic fairy tales were retold in numerous languages." Bolin shrugged and looked toward the parking lot as a familiar van pulled in.

I shouldn't have felt a zing of excitement at Duncan's appearance, especially when I'd been debating his likelihood of thieving thirty seconds earlier, but I caught myself smiling.

A plumbing truck rolled into the parking lot after him—the guys we'd called to fix the pipe leak in our tenant's moldy apartment—and I headed out to meet them. I would have to deal with work first.

"Man the phones and answer emails, will you?" I called over my shoulder to Bolin.

"Like a dutiful secretary instead of an accountant with a college degree and numerous extracurricular activities?"

"Yup."

"Okay."

"Your parents will be pleased."

Bolin grumbled something under his breath but stepped into

the office. What an odd intern. How could the kid believe in druids but not werewolves?

As I led the plumbers to the appropriate apartment, a whistling Duncan hopped out of the sliding door in his van with his metal detector in hand. *He* didn't have bags under his eyes. If he depended on coffee to wake up on a gray Seattle morning, he'd already had it, because he cheerfully waved the metal detector at me before brazenly going over the lawn right in front of the leasing office. Well, I *had* given my permission for that.

After I got the plumbers started, I joined him, standing on the walkway and watching him wander through the dewy grass, shoes growing wet as he swung the metal detector back and forth.

"I chatted with the local alchemist last night," he offered.

"Oh?" An unexpected mixture of anticipation and dread made my gut squirm.

I *wanted* a new stash of my potions. At least I was fairly certain I did. At the same time, Mom's invitation floated through my mind. *If you come hunt with the pack, perhaps you will find what you seek.*

If only I dared. If Augustus and Marco were indicators of how most of the family felt about me, hunting with them would be dangerous. Hell, even turning into a werewolf after twenty-five years of sublimating the magic could be dangerous. What if my temper and ability to control those powerful animal emotions was as bad as it had been back then? Or worse?

"She's going to search for a formula and get back to me soon," Duncan said. "She didn't think it would take long. She has a lot of grimoires and cookbooks—whatever potions recipe books are called—on her shelves. Along with shrunken skulls, bundles of dried herbs, and decorations made with desiccated chicken feet. Her home is a quirky place."

"Says the werewolf who lives in a van decorated with giant magnets and magic detectors. I'm surprised you sleep in there with that stuff. Don't you worry about all that equipment unraveling your DNA or something?"

"Magnets aren't *radioactive*. And the van isn't decorated with them. It stores them for everyday use."

"Which isn't quirky."

"Nope. It's useful, and so am I. As you'll see when I deliver your potion to you at cost plus ten percent."

"That sounds reasonable."

"As I strive to be, my lady." Duncan swept the metal detector out wide so he could bow to me.

One of the plumbers leaned out of the apartment to call, "I turned off the water to replace pipes, but there's a leak in the sewer line too. You need to let me in to the upstairs place to cut their water off too, or you could have shit flooding this place."

"There's a reason I'm bemused when you call me *my lady*," I told Duncan before heading off to help the plumbers.

When I returned, Duncan was waiting for me, the metal detector stationary as he leaned on it, hands folded on top. "There's something else the alchemist wanted to know."

"What?" I asked warily, afraid I would have to further explain why I wanted such a potion.

"Apparently, she knows—or knew—the alchemist who lived and worked here. An old retired nurse and witch, right? This lady wanted to know what happened to her."

"I haven't figured that out yet. Beatrice disappeared from her apartment. So did her furnishings and whatever desiccated doodads she had. I left a message for the only number I have on file—her daughter's, I think—but I haven't been able to get in touch with her or any other relatives."

"Oh. Hmm. This alchemist—Rue is her name—was concerned that there might have been foul play. Or that you or someone else threatened or harmed the other lady. She had some reservations about getting involved with you."

"I don't harm tenants." I didn't try to hide the indignation in my voice. "I work hard and at all hours of the day and night to make sure they're well cared for."

"Oh, I assumed so." Duncan looked toward the apartment where the plumbers worked. "I just didn't know anything about the missing alchemist or what to tell this one."

"I don't know either. Having Beatrice disappear from under my nose is odd. People usually give notice if they're moving out. They want their damage deposits back and for me to stop billing them."

"Naturally." Duncan scratched his jaw. "I'll assure Ms. Rue that you didn't do anything, but... is it possible foul play *was* at work?"

"Beatrice was seventy-five and quilted when she wasn't brewing potions. I can ask some of the local witches, but I doubt she had a lot of enemies left alive."

"*You* seem to have enemies."

"No kidding," I replied automatically before twigging to what he meant. "Wait, you think someone got rid of Beatrice because she was my potion supplier?"

Could Augustus have known about her?

"Maybe someone wanted you to run out," Duncan said.

"I don't think that makes sense. If anything, my enemies—as far as I know, it's really only some family members who are peeved with me—would prefer to keep me in this weaker form." I waved to my human body. "I'd be able to better fend them off if I lost my ability to sublimate the wolf." I wasn't sure when I'd started to speak with Duncan openly about this, but, after turning wolf himself and battling my family, it wasn't as if he hadn't learned quite a bit already.

"I suppose that's true. It was just a thought."

"My ex-husband..." I trailed off, less interested in sharing about Chad.

Duncan raised his eyebrows.

"Never mind," I said.

"Would he have plotted with someone to make you turn into a wolf? You implied his behavior is, ah, sketchy."

"He's an ass. And there's nothing wrong with your memory, is there?"

"Nope."

"I guess the magnets aren't deleterious to your health, after all."

"No, I snuggle right up to them in bed when I'm bereft of female companionship."

"Charming. As to the rest, Chad didn't know about Beatrice. And he's long gone anyway."

"Of course."

"Let me know when I can get the potion, please. I'll be happy to pay your ten percent surcharge." A thought occurred to me, and I leaned into the office, delving into one of the drawers where I stashed chocolate. "Here. A bonus for your hard work." I broke off a number of squares from one of my treasured dark-chocolate bars.

"Oh." Duncan brightened and stepped closer. "Does that one have bits of pork in it too? I wasn't expecting to find meat in chocolate."

"We Americans like to put bacon in everything. We're a health-conscious nation."

"Yes, quite. I believe that's what the rest of the world knows this country for."

"I have no doubt."

Duncan snorted, but he accepted the squares.

"Those are orange dark chocolate. They're meatless but good. Bring me that potion at only five percent above cost, and I'll make you one of my famous desserts. My boys love it. Chocolate-covered beef jerky rolled in honey-toasted pecans. It's also popular with..."

A tenant walked out the door and headed toward the parking lot, glancing our way.

I finished with, "carnivores," instead of *werewolves.*

When I turned to head into the office, Duncan stopped me with a questioning, "Luna?"

"Yes?"

"Tomorrow's the full moon."

"I'm aware." I didn't and wouldn't mention the increasingly strong urges I'd been experiencing these last few nights.

Duncan glanced back to make sure the tenant was out of earshot. "Would you like to go for a hunt with me tonight?"

My belly fluttered with nerves. He was asking me on a date. Werewolf-style. This was how our kind did it.

"I mean, if you can," Duncan added. "Er, *can* you? If you haven't gotten that potion yet, you could be... you, right?"

You could be *you.* As if I'd been an inauthentic person my entire adult life. I knew he hadn't meant it as an insult, but I couldn't help but wince.

"Not that we couldn't hunt if you were human," he added, maybe noticing my reaction. "I don't have anything vested in seeing you change. It's just that I didn't notice any guns in your apartment. I'd guess you would have trouble bringing down a ten-point buck as a human."

"I do have that reciprocating saw."

"If you bring that along on a hunt and try to stab a deer with it... I would feel fully justified in recording the confrontation to upload to my social-media sites." Duncan tapped the phone in his pocket.

"Aren't you and your silvering pelt a little old for social media?"

"My pelt is merely *highlighted* by silver right now, and of course not. I have to document my magnet-fishing and metal-detecting adventures."

"People get excited seeing you pluck rusty forks out of lakes?"

"Oh yes. It's the accent, you see. Bacon isn't the only thing you Americans love." He winked at me.

"Uh-huh." I turned, intending to get to work, but he stopped me with another prompt.

"A hunt?"

I started to shake my head, but hadn't I been worrying about visiting my family and joining the entire pack for a hunt? And how dangerous that could turn out to be for me? Assuming I could successfully change at all, after all this time, and I didn't yet know if I could.

Going with Duncan the night before the full moon might be a low-key way to test things. To see if I could still change, to see if I had the power and stamina I'd once claimed, enough to take down a buck—or another predator turning on me. I could go on my own, but if something went wrong... maybe it wouldn't be a bad idea to have someone friendly around to help. Oh, I still didn't trust that Duncan wasn't here on a personal agenda, but I didn't get the vibe that he intended me any harm. Not like my awful cousin. Duncan had *protected* me from Augustus. From all of them. Maybe Duncan wanted something from me, and it would be easier to get if I was alive, but maybe he actually liked me.

"Okay," I said, the nerves once more teasing my gut.

"Excellent." Duncan bowed to me again, popped some chocolate into his mouth, and fired up his metal detector. "I'll see you tonight."

I hoped I wouldn't regret my decision.

15

AFTER THE OFFICE HOURS ENDED, THE PLUMBERS WERE GONE, THREE locked-out tenants had been let in, and Bolin had gone home for the day, I turned to the computer to look up Duncan online. Since he'd given me his full name, I could have researched him before, but it hadn't crossed my mind until he'd mentioned having social-media sites.

The Duncan Caldwells that came up didn't match my lone wolf, leading me to wonder if that was truly his name. Then I typed in the text on his van, which I assumed was his business name, if he *had* a legitimate business. *Full Moon Fortune Hunter.*

"There we go," I murmured as social-media sites popped up, with YouTube at the top.

I opened videos for a channel that showed Duncan, with his beard stubble and wavy, jaw-length gray-shot hair, fishing items out of lakes, canals, ponds, and rivers. A highlighted video showed him in front of a castle, holding a sword aloft.

"Well, better than a fork."

After watching a couple of videos and surfing back far enough to verify that he'd been doing this for years, I poked through links, searching for a useful *about me* section. But what I could find didn't offer much, merely saying he'd been raised in the United Kingdom and traveled the world, seeking adventure—and people's lost belongings. There was nothing about his rates, about how to hire him, or about what kinds of things he found for his clients.

Most of the videos showed him locating mundane objects, some with historical significance, but I did find a couple of older ones where he was roaming dark forests—and more than a few cemeteries—with his *magic detector*. A few blurry apparitions, or something of that ilk, appeared and disappeared in the background. Not surprisingly, those videos had the most views. People did love the paranormal.

"But don't believe in werewolves." I remembered Bolin's statement with bemusement.

Of all the people I would expect to be a believer...

A knock on the door startled me. Feeling guilty for my research, I closed the browser window before answering.

"There you are," Duncan said.

"Here I am."

"You look..." He eyed the attire I'd chosen for the night. "Comfortable."

Did that mean I looked homely?

Crossing my arms over my chest, I said, "Sweatpants and hoodies are easy to remove in a pinch. I'm not so wealthy that I can afford to buy new clothes every time I change too abruptly to remove them in time."

"That's what I do. Takes the stress out of jeans fasteners that are hard to unbutton quickly."

"You must be raking in the YouTube ad revenue."

His eyes gleamed. "You checked out my channel? I'm touched by your interest."

"I like to research weirdos before I get in a van with them." I looked toward the parking lot, assuming he meant to drive us out somewhere to hunt, not hope to get lucky with opossums and raccoons in the wetlands between houses in Shoreline.

"That does seem wise." Duncan extended a hand toward his vehicle. "In preparation for our evening, I cleaned off the passenger seat and ensured no large and powerful magnets are close enough to scramble your DNA."

I pointed at him. "I *knew* that was a possibility."

"Only if you eat a lot of iron." He smirked and turned toward the parking lot.

I grabbed a bag with my purse, keys, phone, and a change of clothes—just in case. I was not riding home *naked* in a van with him. I'd also packed my reciprocating saw and a huge pipe wrench. Mostly to amuse him, but one never knew. If I couldn't change, and we ran into my family, I didn't want to be defenseless.

The inside of the van smelled like cleaning solution and machine oil. I peeked back at a tiny bed and kitchen area amid racks of equipment, including the SCUBA gear I'd glimpsed before. Coils of rope, insulated boxes, and a sturdy safe occupied all the space under the bed. If there was a closet or anyplace for all the clothes he supposedly purchased for unplanned changes, I couldn't see it from the front.

I eased onto the passenger seat, hoping I wasn't being a fool for going off with a strange man. Though we'd had a lot of conversations in the last few days, it wasn't as if I'd known him long.

"Please enjoy the refreshing beverage I brought for you." Before sliding into the driver's seat, he fished into a cooler and withdrew two chilled cans of soda. "It's an American staple, I understand."

"Diet Coke?" I accepted a can and tucked it into the holder. "Beer might be better for taking the edge off."

"I've found it isn't a good idea to change while inebriated."

"The authorities frown on that while driving too."

"Indeed."

He'd cleared the seat but not the seat well, so I had to prop my feet on toolboxes, heavy bags, and who knew what else that was piled under the glovebox.

"Can you recommend a good place to hunt?" Duncan closed his door and started the van. It was old enough to take a key in the ignition.

"You don't want to settle for opossums and raccoons in the neighborhood parks?"

He gave me an aggrieved look. "If I wanted to do that, I could change in the bushes behind your apartment complex."

"The tenants appreciate that you're not making that choice. The fight with my cousins was bad enough. You're lucky Animal Control didn't show up with tranquilizer guns."

They *had* come the morning after, sans guns, as far as I'd seen. The tenant who'd called them hadn't been home to tell stories of wolves, so I'd pointed the officers to the greenbelt and mentioned coyotes. They *did* wander into the city and scavenge in the parks and wetlands from time to time.

"Quite."

"Head east toward the mountains." I gave him directions to the nearest freeway access point. Since my family lived to the north and might well be out hunting tonight too, east would be safer.

"Are we likely to run into your pack out there?" Duncan might have been thinking about the same thing. Though he'd beaten my cousin when they'd fought one-on-one, the encounter had grown dicier when more of the family had shown up.

I didn't blame him for not wanting to get ganged up on again. "Hopefully not."

He gave me a long look but nodded. "Right. Good."

As he drove off, I realized he also had to trust me. Might he be nervous about that? Presumably, I was as much a stranger to him as he was to me. If he'd known about my past, he might not have invited me out into the forest alone.

That thought made a tendril of concern curl through me. I'd been worrying about going off alone with him, but if I was still the same person—the same *werewolf*—I had been all those years ago, I could be as much a danger to him as he was to me. I'd loved Raoul, but when he'd roused my temper, I'd lost it, the wolf turning into a savage and uncontrollable animal.

What if that happened again? I didn't have strong feelings for Duncan. It might be easier to lose my temper with him, to give in to my lupine instincts and forget he was an ally. I wasn't even positive he *was* an ally.

"Maybe we shouldn't hunt together," I blurted, that concern settling like a cannonball in my gut.

Though he was focused on navigating traffic that hadn't diminished with the coming of night, he managed a thoughtful look over at me. "Are you worried about being alone with me?"

"Yeah, but probably not for the reason you think."

"That a lack of restraint in your lupine form will cause you to fling yourself on me in an amorous fashion?"

"*That's* what you thought would happen tonight?"

"I don't know about you, but the chase, followed by a feast, has been known to make *me* amorous."

"You're a guy. Doesn't everything make you amorous?"

"Not as much as when I was younger, but things do trend that way. As to the hunt, I'd thought you might enjoy going together. I get the impression, well, if your children and your ex-husband are fully human, and you're estranged from your werewolf family, and you've been taking that potion for a long time... It must have been a while since you hunted with someone, no? I thought you might enjoy some company."

"I guess." I chewed on the inside of my cheek and debated if I should warn him that I'd killed before—and not only prey. It would be hard to do that without speaking of Raoul's death.

"Such enthusiasm." Duncan laughed without rancor. "I always hated enforced solitude, but maybe you prefer it."

"Not necessarily. You're right that I haven't hunted with anyone in a long time, but I have some concerns." I rubbed my thighs through my sweatpants, reluctant to speak about my past but feeling less vulnerable than usual in the darkened van, the shadows hiding the emotions on my face.

"How long has it been since you changed?" he asked.

"I was nineteen when I left the pack. I'm forty-five now."

Duncan gaped at me, the lights of the dash revealing his open mouth. "You haven't changed in twenty-six years?"

"I've taken the potion faithfully since I found out it existed and that I could buy it."

"But *why*? Did your husband require it? I can get wanting to fit in, maybe—" his expression said he did *not* get it, "—but to give up all that you are..."

"Being a wild animal is not *all that I am*. It never was, and it wasn't about fitting in."

Duncan lifted a hand from the steering wheel. "No, and I didn't mean to offend. It's just that... Well, I enjoy the hunts, the time spent in nature with the magic enhancing my senses. I love the pure joy of running, the feel of the earth under my paws, and the smells of damp foliage and the musk of one's prey. It's all... It's what's *real*. At least to me. Everything is more genuine when I'm a wolf. I've learned to appreciate my time as a man, but when the call comes, I have no hesitation to accept it."

"I'm glad you've got it all figured out," I said stiffly and looked out the window. I clamped my mouth shut, sublimating the urge to explain further, to *defend* myself. I hadn't wanted to share any of my past with him, and I didn't know how that had happened.

"It's more that I've learned to accept that which is unchangeable in my wise old age." Duncan snorted softly, his focus on the freeway. We'd left the city, and the lights of the suburbs were growing sparser, with the forested mountains looming ahead of us. "If I had it all figured out, maybe I would have a family instead of being a lone wolf."

"Did you have a pack back in the Old World?"

"No."

"Did you challenge an alpha and get driven out?"

That was how it usually happened, at least that I'd observed. And most lone wolves didn't end up living long. They often tried to integrate fully into human civilization, much as I had, but ended up feeling the call, changing, and going on hunts alone. Sometimes, that worked out. Sometimes, it didn't... And when they woke, gored by antlers, there was no one to care for them, to bring them to a wise wolf for healing, and they passed alone in the forest.

"I never got that opportunity." His tone turned dry. "Had I challenged an alpha, I might have won. You've seen my exquisite physique." He flexed a biceps, though it would have been his physique as a wolf that would have mattered in a pack fight.

"It was all right."

Duncan *had* been a big wolf—and magnificent. Alone, he would have kicked Augustus's ass. I had little doubt.

"All right?" He sniffed. "Really, my lady."

"I was too distracted by the lushness of your silvering pelt to notice your overall fitness."

Duncan squinted suspiciously over at me. "At least *something* of mine captured your attention."

"I'm a fan of lushness." I smiled. This was safer to talk about than the past.

"Should we ever succumb to our immense physical attraction to each other and end up rutting with abandon in the forest, I won't be offended if I wake in your arms with you stroking my pelt."

"Assuming there *was* physical attraction, I usually rut in my bedroom as a human."

"*Usually*. There must have been a time when you were a horny wolf. The teenage years are particularly libido-fueled, as I remember."

Not answering the question, I said, "If I lived in a van, I'd probably prefer the woods too."

"My van *does* have a bed."

"If it's as cramped as this passenger seat—" I lifted one of my legs, my knee getting stiff from my foot being propped on boxes, "—I can't imagine you've lured many women into it."

"You might be surprised. If I sought to lure *you*, I suspect I could accomplish that mission by tossing a couple of squares of chocolate onto the bed back there."

"You'd better make it a whole bar." I looked into the dark back of the van, though the shadows hid the bed. "Maybe a *box* of bars."

"I'll keep that in mind. The kind with bacon bits, right?"

"Honey-bourbon bacon bits." I pointed at a sign alongside the freeway. "Take the next exit. We can hunt back there."

"Together? Or separately?" He hadn't forgotten the comment that started the conversation.

I sighed. "Let's... see how it goes, I guess. How many miles to the gallon does your van get?"

Duncan blinked at the change in topic.

I delved into my purse while calculating the length of the journey. "About twenty? Fifteen?"

"Yeah, it's not a lot. Especially when the van is driven off road, into parks, and used as a battering ram to send enemies flying." Duncan sounded more pleased than upset about that.

"I had no idea it had such a finicky engine and that such activities would affect its average MPG." I opened my GAS envelope, pulled out six dollars, and laid the bills on the dashboard for him.

"Is that a tip for services you expect me to render later?"

"It's my contribution to tonight's gas money."

"That's not necessary." Duncan peered toward my purse. "How many envelopes are there?"

I closed it. "Enough."

"Huh."

He didn't *say* I was weird, but I'd heard it before, so I had no trouble interpreting that grunt. I ignored it, as I'd learned to do. The hell with what anyone thought. My budgeting had gotten me out of debt, and I intended to have an investment property of my own within the next few years.

As we took the exit, the clouds parted, and the nearly full moon shone down upon us. Of its own accord, my body shifted toward that light, almost straining at the seat belt. My blood sang, and my nerves fired with the longing to change.

I'd worried that I might not be able to after all this time, that the lingering effects of the potion would keep me human, but my entire body ached with the need to answer the moon's call. I yearned to yank off my clothes, spring into the woods, and let the wolf overtake me.

Duncan looked over at me, the moonlight gleaming in his eyes, and I knew he felt the same thing. He nodded at me. Tonight, we would hunt.

16

WE DIDN'T MAKE IT FAR FROM THE FREEWAY EXIT BEFORE DUNCAN stopped the van on a bridge that crossed over a shallow river, a sign for a trailhead on the far side. This late in the day, there weren't any cars parked there, but we could make out lights in the town on the other side of the freeway, and I could hear traffic noise.

"We might want to go farther up the mountain for a more peaceful hunt," I said.

"Oh, I've no doubt, but I sensed something, and this is such a likely spot."

"A likely spot for what?"

Duncan grinned as he pointed at a sidewalk to one side of the road that crossed the bridge, then turned off the ignition and slipped into the back of the van. A couple of clunks and a click sounded before he hopped out the side door with one of his huge magnets on a rope. He also carried a pole with a net at the top. It looked like a modified pool strainer. And was that his magic detector, as well?

Whistling cheerfully, Duncan leaned the tools against the

railing and pointed the magic detector at the river. A soft beeping reached my ears.

"Hah," he said in triumph, then trotted off the bridge and down to the bank. He thrust his net into the water and started fishing around for whatever he'd detected.

Judging this might take a while, I climbed out of the van. A car heading down from the mountain appeared, the passengers looking curiously at Duncan as they drove across the bridge. He, I decided with certainty, was weird too.

"Is this how *you* pay for gas?" I asked.

"Most certainly. Food, gas, and van maintenance."

"Do you pay taxes on what you earn from what you find?"

"I'm not a citizen."

"Even in the UK?"

"I grew up somewhat off-the-grid."

I side-eyed him at that. "So, no taxes?"

"I don't even exist, as far as the government is concerned."

"Mysterious."

"Oh, I am. Toss the magnet in if you like," Duncan offered as he continued to fish about in the area his detector had drawn him to. "Magical stuff isn't *usually* magnetic, but sometimes it is."

The moon called to my blood, and testing my ability to change and hunt was more on my mind than fishing in a river for rusty forks or whatever treasure he sought. But, since he'd driven, I felt obligated to be patient. To humor him, I hefted the cylindrical magnet and tossed it off the bridge to land near where he was probing. It splashed water up on Duncan on the bank.

"Thank you," he said dryly.

"You're welcome. I can't imagine you get to shower often when living in a van."

"Are you judging me for my lifestyle, my lady?"

"Just the part where you avoid paying taxes."

"But the other parts are acceptable?" He waggled his eyebrows at me.

"They're okay."

"Your praise and approval warm my cockles."

"What's a cockle?" I'd heard the phrase but not in a long time. "Something they have in the UK?"

"For sure." Duncan gestured at the rope.

As I'd seen him do, I used it to drag the magnet along the bottom of the stream. Rocks and uneven ground made it difficult to pull, and I imagined the hobby being much easier along a canal. Surprisingly, when I pulled the magnet out of the water, a few items stuck to it. I hadn't expected anything magnetic in a mountain stream, though I supposed people walked over the bridge, stopped to take pictures of the scenic waterway, and accidentally dropped things in.

"Will these car keys cover a lot of gas money?" I plucked a set off, the metal ring stuck so strongly to the powerful magnet that it was a challenge.

"Probably only if we find the car they go with."

"What is this?" I murmured, sensing something.

As I reached for a flat oval stuck to the magnet, the magic detector resting next to me started beeping. Startled, I almost dropped everything.

"Ah, is that it?" With the pole in hand, Duncan trotted back up to the bridge.

Covered in grime, the oval had a tiny ring on one end. It was a hook to attach it to a necklace, I realized. The chain was long gone, but it was a pendant or maybe a locket. I scraped at the slimy coating, trying to figure out if it could be opened.

A flash of intuition came over me, startling me anew. It was almost a *vision*, something I'd never experienced before. In it, I saw the river lit by sun and lined by trees with leaves that were still green. A gray-haired lady in a dress and shawl stood on the bridge.

On the railing in front of her, a fat hardback book lay open. As she read from it, she gripped the locket where it hung around her neck. From a pocket, she withdrew a mixture of powders and sprinkled them in the water. Blue light shone through her fingers and highlighted her weathered face, and she leaned back, as if basking in the glow. Some of the age lines and weariness—or maybe that was pain—on her face lessened as the light faded, and she lowered her hand.

"Oh, a longevity talisman." Duncan pointed to the find. "I've seen them before. Talented witches who've studied alchemy and metallurgy can make them."

The vision, if that was what it had been, faded, and I held the gewgaw out at arm's length. Had I seen an actual event from the past? One that gave me a glimpse into what the magical item did? If so, that was the first time anything like that had happened to me. Of course, it was the first time I'd held a supposed longevity talisman. I'd never heard of them.

"I don't think there's any proof that they *really* make the owner live longer." Duncan was studying it instead of me, probably unaware of my vision. "But they're reputed to help with the pain of arthritis and gout and other conditions, at least for a time. They might even speed up healing. Such a find could be worth money to the right person. To *many* people." He touched his ribs where my cousins had gouged him and grimaced.

"I wonder how it was lost."

Had a car come barreling through and hit the woman—the witch?—as she'd been calling upon the talisman's power?

"People drop things in the water all the time." Duncan shrugged. "I wouldn't have a career otherwise."

"You consider what you do a career, huh?"

"Indeed! One full of adventure, travel, and intrigue. And I hardly ever have to carry toilets around." He winked to soften any dig he felt he'd made about my job.

Since I'd been digging at his, I couldn't feel insulted. "I guess your work has romantic aspects."

"Quite. I've had pirates attempt to rob me on three separate occasions."

That wasn't as romantic as I'd imagined, and I raised skeptical eyebrows. "Are you sure that's better than doing apartment repairs?"

"Oh yes. I fought them off twice. It was only a band of well-armed and organized Gulf of Guinea pirates that were too much for even a werewolf to handle. I had to dive overboard, swim to shore with a bullet in my shoulder, and wait until the authorities were available to help me find the remains of the boat I'd rented. Fortunately, the insurance somewhat covered the losses. Pirates are more common than you'd think."

"Your story not only makes me certain that my job is better than yours, but it has me inclined to snuggle up to the next toilet I install." I handed him the locket, trusting he knew how to properly clean it and find a buyer who knew its worth. If there was a magical-items pawn shop in the Seattle area, I had no idea where.

"That makes for an interesting mental picture." Duncan accepted the locket with a nod. "I'll send you half of whatever I get when I sell this."

"That's not necessary."

"It's as necessary as the gas money." He gave me a frank look.

I wasn't sure the two things were comparable but said, "Okay," instead of objecting further.

After he returned his gear to his van, he held open the passenger door for me with a deep bow. "We can continue our date now."

"You're weirder than I am, I think."

"Oh, I don't doubt that." Duncan didn't exactly *skip* back to the driver's side, but his body language promised he was enjoying the night.

Well, he was a better date than my ex-husband had been. No doubt about that.

As he drove farther from the highway, I mulled over the significance of the vision. I'd heard of people who experienced such things—the internet was rife with stories of such paranormal experiences. Supposedly, that was how witches, druids, and the like sometimes first learned of their potential to use magic. But werewolves didn't have *visions*. At least I didn't think so. What if this was some ability that I'd been inadvertently suppressing, along with all my lupine senses, over the years with my potions?

Maybe, if I returned to Monroe for the pack hunt, I could ask my mother if anyone in the family had such experiences. Not that it really mattered. How often did I come in contact with magical artifacts?

I'd no sooner had the thought than the case from my bedroom came to mind. Lately, magical artifacts abounded around me.

17

On a dirt road a couple of miles from the freeway, the rumble of traffic having faded, Duncan stopped his van. He rolled down the window and sniffed into the night air. Hoping to catch the whiff of interesting animals to hunt?

Though I doubted I'd detect any animal scents while in human form, I rolled down my own window. The smell of loamy earth, decaying leaves, water from a nearby creek, and a promise of rain filled the air. If the musky odors of any animals lingered, I couldn't pick them up.

Duncan inhaled deeply. "Invigorating, isn't it?"

"It is." I remembered him touching his ribs and asked, "How are your wounds doing? They won't slow you down during a hunt, will they?"

"Certainly not. As I told you, I heal quickly." Duncan opened his door and slid out. "I was especially fortunate to have the tender ministrations of a beautiful lady to help along the process."

"I didn't know my half-ass cleaning of your wound and handing you the bandage to wrap it yourself counted as tender." I would have done more if we hadn't been interrupted, but he'd seemed experienced at performing first-aid on himself.

"I refer to the gentle way you stroked me after the battle."

"You remember that, huh?"

"I do. It was delightful."

"Well, your fur was... lush."

"As we've established." Duncan drew his shirt over his head, tossed it onto his seat, then bent to tug off his shoes.

It made sense to disrobe, so your clothes didn't disappear in the magic of the change, but I caught myself watching him instead of getting out of the van and doing the same. His powerful shoulder and back muscles shifted and flexed as he tugged off his shoes and socks. I'd thought I was long past caring that much about men or being interested in sex, but his appealing physique made me speculate about touching him.

Duncan looked up, catching me observing him.

Cheeks warming, I looked away.

"I can go into the woods to change and wait for you if you want privacy," he said, not commenting on my gaze. "Or do you think it might take a while? I... can't imagine not changing for decades. Or taking a drug to keep the call from coming over me."

"Yeah." I couldn't disagree that it was an unusual choice for a werewolf. "It's possible that after all this time, I won't even be able to do it. Or there may be enough potion lingering in me to stop it." I shrugged, but I believed I'd be able to turn into the wolf. These last couple of days, it had tried to surge up in me a number of times.

"I can bring you back some choice morsels from a fresh kill if you're not able to hunt on your own."

"Thoughtful." I couldn't imagine gnawing on a raw liver, or whatever he had in mind, in my human form.

"You've been kind enough to supply me with all those delicious squares of chocolate."

Once fully undressed, he padded off the road and into the woods. The moonlight shone on his pale butt cheeks, and I almost laughed.

The moonlight also shone through the windshield and onto my face. Its power made my skin tingle. The wolf magic bubbled within me, as if it had been waiting for ages for an opportunity to escape. Out here in the woods, with the moon beaming down on me, the wolf didn't hesitate to make itself known. It wanted out. It wanted to hunt.

Afraid of losing my clothing, I hopped out of the van and hurried to remove my shoes, socks, sweatpants, hoodie, and T-shirt. I felt the cool autumn night air on my skin, the grit of the dirt road under my feet, and the caress of a breeze that raised gooseflesh. But the chill faded as my body flushed with heat—with *magic*—from the moon and from within. As I tugged off my undergarments, the scents of the forest grew much more vibrant, and I could pick out individual odors and knew what made them and what animals and people had passed this way. I smelled the wolf in the area—Duncan—and knew he hadn't gone far.

When I looked into the trees, my eyes much sharper now, I picked him out of the shadows. He sat on his haunches, watching the road, his pointed ears rotating now and then at noises in the forest.

My skin pricked and a delicious stretching sensation filled me as I changed, body morphing, fur sprouting, and magic rippling through me. The world shifted, and I dropped to all fours. For the first time in twenty-six years, I was a wolf.

And, for the first time in twenty-six years, I caught the scents of wild animals, of ducks in a nearby pond, of squirrels bedded down in the branches of a pine, and of... ah, deer. Several of them. That was prey suitable for a wolf, and I salivated at the thought of taking one down, of consuming it.

When I'd been human, I hadn't been hungry, but the wolf was

always hungry. It longed to feast, to feed the body and the magic, enough to last until the next full moon, the next hunt.

Letting my nose lead me, I loped off in the direction of the deer. With my senses heightened, I wasn't surprised when another wolf joined me, running at my side. He wasn't family, not of the pack, but his tongue lolled out, and he regarded me in a friendly manner. I knew him from the other life, didn't I? Yes. He would be an ally on the hunt.

Side-by-side, we ran through a gully where grass had grown verdant and high over the summer. In the past, the native trees had been logged by humans, enough to allow moonlight down to bathe the ground. A stream meandered through the center of the gully. With food and drink for the deer, it was an ideal place for them.

We passed a few mushrooms that, to my lupine eyes, glowed in the dark. They were magical. As a wolf, it was not only my eyes and ears that were keener, but I could detect otherworldly elements that were invisible to humans.

A memory flashed in my mind. An ivory case with a wolf engraved on the lid. Like the mushrooms, it also had magic, powerful magic.

A case made by a two-legs was a strange thing for a predator on the hunt to think about, and confusion trickled through me, but I vowed to remember the moment later. A certainty spread, pushing aside the confusion, that I would find the case enlightening to examine when I was in my wolf form.

I glimpsed a deer, and more important thoughts surged to the forefront of my mind.

Like the squirrels, the herd was bedded down for the night. We approached from downwind, trying to mask our scents. In the end, the deer would notice us, and we would have to run, as we enjoyed doing, but we had to get close first. These animals had long legs and were as fast as we, sometimes faster.

The other wolf left me to approach their resting place from the far side of the gully. Yes, we would flank them, making it harder for them to escape. I slowed from a lope to a stalk, padding silently through the grass, using bushes and old logs to hide my approach.

One deer stood near the stream, watching for threats as the rest of its herd slept. It was a buck of three or four years, and it would be a challenge to catch him off-guard and bring him down. If winter had been deep, and I'd been hungrier, I would have targeted the old deer, those easier to catch, but my blood sang under the silvery moonlight, and I wanted a challenge.

The buck's head rose high, nostrils in the air. Had he caught our scent?

He waved his short tail and blew forcibly through his nostrils, a *whoosh, whoosh*. Yes, he sensed danger. Others in the herd stirred, rising from their grassy beds. Soon, they would bolt.

A faint rustle from the far side of the gully reached my ears. The other wolf. He'd given up stealth to sprint at the deer. The buck snorted and stomped to warn the others, then turned to run.

I also abandoned stealth and charged after them. No, after the buck. My chosen prey.

Powerful muscles flexing, I ran, covering ground fast, heading straight for that buck. The other wolf angled in, also running fast. He was as strong as I and headed toward a slower doe that had seen many years, but he noticed my target and, tongue lolling out again, he altered his course. Together, we sprinted after the buck.

It ran fast, springing over mossy logs and boulders, but we closed on it. We parted enough to flank it, me on the left and the other wolf on the right. He sprang first, going for one of its fore-limbs to bring it down. The buck lurched sideways, trying to escape the crush of lupine jaws. It veered right into me. I leaped for its throat, tearing deep, landing the blow that would end its life. It crumpled, giving itself so two wolves could feast, as the call of the moon commanded them to do.

The exhilaration of the hunt flowed through me, invigorating, and the world all about was sharp and real as we dined. The moon shone upon our backs, our thick fur gleaming in the light. All seemed right and natural. When we were sated, we padded away, leaving the rest for the scavengers in the forest, those birds and animals who lacked the power of wolves.

Across the stream, we settled among ferns to rest and digest. Eventually, I dozed and dreamed, not in color as I did as a human but in the silver of moonlight. I ran through the forest and came to a clearing, and that case lay in the middle, glowing faintly in invitation.

18

Before dawn, with the sky starting to lighten, I woke in my normal human body, naked and lying on trampled fern fronds. There was a hand on my boob.

I blinked, eyeing that as I processed the warmth of an arm wrapped around me and an equally naked male body pressed against my back. I turned my head to look at Duncan. His eyes were closed, his breathing even with sleep.

Given how chilly the predawn air was, I wouldn't have minded snuggling for warmth, but the hand was a little presumptuous. Making a face, I grasped it to move it off my chest. His arm tightened around me, and he snuggled closer, lips brushing my bare shoulder. A tingle of warmth swept through me, promising that, even though I'd not been with a man since before my husband left, my body remembered how to respond to an appealing touch.

But Duncan was still a mystery, and I didn't want to find his touch appealing.

"We're not a couple, dude." I sat up and shoved his arm off.

His eyes opened, and he looked blearily up at me.

"I should have known you'd be the handsy type," I told him.

Whether he'd known he'd been groping me or not, it wasn't clear, but he smiled without shame. "You were magnificent."

"I assume you mean on the hunt since nothing else happened."

His smile widened.

Alarm flashed through me. Hell, nothing *had* happened, had it?

I remembered falling asleep, still in my lupine form, and dreaming of that case. There hadn't been any sex, not as a wolf or as a human. I was positive. *Almost* positive. The werewolf magic often made memories of what happened while in lupine form fuzzy. Just as, when I was a wolf, memories of my human life could also be harder to grasp and process.

"On the hunt," Duncan said, taking pity on me and clarifying. "I didn't realize how sleek and powerful you would be. You're bigger than your brutish cousins. If you would let yourself change whenever they troubled you..."

"I told you why I don't."

"Actually, you were quite vague about that and *didn't* tell me. What happened to you? I saw your beauty and soul as a wolf, the exhilaration you felt being on the hunt. It was just as powerful as what I experience. How could you turn your back on that? On your nature and what you were born to be?"

"It's none of your business." I stood, brushing off dirt and fern fronds. Maybe I was odd, but his questions made me bristle more than waking up with his hand on my boob had.

"Okay." Duncan shrugged easily and stood up, revealing that he'd probably been dreaming of something besides wolf cases while he'd had his arm wrapped around me.

I looked away, not wanting to gawk at him and have him believe I was interested. But he caught my glance and grinned, standing proudly, not trying to hide anything.

"I need to be back at the apartment complex by the time office hours begin." I hoped he knew how to find the van again.

As a wolf, it would have been a simple matter to follow our scent trail back to it, but my human nose lacked such sensitivity. Though, in the aftermath of the change, the world did seem sharper, the air currents laden with far more odors than I usually noticed.

"Does that mean you don't want to see if we're as good together in bed as we were on the hunt?" Duncan had politely been gazing at my face, but at that comment, he glanced lower. Lust and appreciation glinted in his eyes before he looked away, dropping a mask over his interest.

Maybe I should have chastised him for the glance, but I caught myself feeling pleased. With two grown sons, I'd thought I was past the age where men would want to ogle my naked body. Now and then, out in public, I got looks, but Chad's cheating had left me feeling beaten and broken—and that my attractiveness had long since faded.

"There aren't any beds out here," was all I said.

"Those ferns weren't bad."

"They were cold, damp, and prickly. Do you know where your van is?"

"Of course." Duncan pointed toward trees at the start of the gully where we'd found the deer.

"Do you know where your *keys* are?"

He tapped his chin thoughtfully. "We'll find out."

We parted long enough to tend to biological needs and drink from the stream. That wasn't something I would usually do in human form, but wolves didn't carry hydration packs, and we'd both already quenched our thirst there the night before.

Afterward, I followed Duncan up the gully. The stream gurgled pleasantly beside us, and birds sang as the sky grew brighter. While we walked, I mulled over the case to take my mind off the rocks and roots scraping the bottoms of my feet. Ambling through the forest was a lot easier with sturdy paw pads than delicate human soles, and I looked forward to dressing.

Duncan glanced back often as we trekked toward the road. Checking to make sure I was keeping up?

Chin up, I ignored the ground poking my feet and kept pace with him. The previous night's vision had me thinking that looking at the case through lupine eyes might reveal something, but I didn't know if I could summon the wolf and then remember that some trifling human object had importance to me. Once I was in lupine form, I would forget my to-do list. Instead, I would take off into the closest wilderness to hunt.

"I get why you don't trust me—nobody ever trusts lone wolves," Duncan said after one of his glances caught me frowning pensively. "But I'll give you my number before I go. It seems like your family has turned against you. If you ever need someone to talk to, I'll listen. I know what it's like to be lonely. Trust me."

"I'm fine. I've been alone a while. I'm used to it." Sort of. Even before I'd kicked Chad out, he'd barely been home. The difference now was that my boys were also gone.

"Being used to being alone doesn't necessarily make it easy."

"Yeah." I decided not to argue. He probably *did* understand better than most. "Thanks for offering," I made myself add, though I doubted I would take him up on it. "When are you leaving? You haven't metal-detected all our acres yet."

Duncan chuckled. "I haven't, no, but the woods were primarily what drew me. There was some magic about." He opened his mouth—to mention the magic we'd found in my apartment?—but shrugged and didn't bring it up. He pointed through the trees, the dirt road and his van visible in the distance. "I'll need to go soon. When I was fighting your cousins, they conveyed that they would come after me again if I stayed in their territory."

He touched the wound on his side. The bandages had disappeared with his change, so I could see that the gashes were healing quickly, thanks to the regenerative power of the wolf. That was good, though they must have hurt when he'd received them.

"That's probably a legitimate threat and not a bluff," I admitted. "There's a reason I had you drive out east instead of north."

"They don't hunt out here?"

"Not as often. Those with cabins in the woods for homes, like my mother, are north of Monroe. There used to be another pack who hunted over this way." I remembered Raoul and the feud with the Cascade Crushers but didn't want to go into it any more than anything else about my past. "My family claimed it after they left, but it's not quite home."

"Understood." Duncan reached the van first and opened the door for me. Our clothes were draped on the seats where we'd left them. "I'm glad they didn't show up on our hunt. I enjoyed being a wolf with you much more than with your cousins."

"Yeah, I thought you were a decent hunting buddy too."

He snorted. "The way you stroke my ego is almost as appealing as the way you stroke my fur."

I couldn't help but laugh, meeting his warm brown eyes as I stepped closer. I lifted a hand, intending to reach past him to grab my clothes, but when our bodies brushed, a zing of awareness swept through me again. The memory of him checking me out came to mind, and I caught myself stepping closer to him instead of the seat. He lifted a hand to my waist, callused palm cupping me.

"You *are* magnificent." His gaze dipped to my lips. "If you want to remain mysterious and never tell me anything about yourself, you can also just call me for a hunt. Anytime."

"Is *hunting* what you really want to do with me?"

Our chests brushed, his taut muscles hard under his warm skin, a spattering of hair making an appealing sensation against my sensitive flesh.

"Among other things." His eyes glinted with humor, humor and a more intense emotion, the same as I'd caught in the woods. Desire. Lust.

He bent toward me, mouth opening slightly, and I leaned closer. Our lips met, warm and gentle and full of a promise of an enjoyable time. I leaned into him, tempted to give in to that. Tempted to—

A howl in the forest made us spring apart. It carried across the wilderness, traveling miles, but my ears were sharper than the day before, sharp enough to know it had originated nearby. The wolf making the noise might even be close enough to see us.

"Anyone you know?" Our moment broken, Duncan jogged around to the driver side of the van and started dressing.

I started to say no, but my keener ears could also pick out subtleties that I couldn't have before. It was a familiar howl, a familiar *voice*. Not one I'd heard in a long time, but...

"I think it's a wolf from my pack." I grabbed my own clothing and started dressing.

"Objecting to our nude closeness or my presence in their woods? Or *your* presence in their woods?" Duncan fished his keys out of his pocket and climbed in, turning the ignition.

The howl sounded again, this time even closer. The wolf was up the road around a bend or two. Was he alone? I imagined my cousins rushing us.

"Maybe all of those things." I jumped inside and closed the door, tugging my trousers up as Duncan turned the van around. "Our nudity is probably the least offensive thing though."

"It certainly didn't offend *me*." He grinned over at me, glancing at my bare thigh before my trousers were fully in place.

"You do seem like someone who would be fully comfortable on a nude beach."

"Naturally." Duncan got the van turned around and headed down the road toward the freeway.

I looked in the side mirror as we departed and wasn't surprised to spot a white wolf watching us from the road. It had been years since I'd seen him, but that was Lorenzo, an older male that had joined our pack decades earlier. He hadn't stayed, leaving before I had, to start a family of his own in Eastern Washington, but something must have drawn him back. He gazed after us with cool blue eyes.

Had he been ordered to watch me? Or had he simply been hunting in the area and detected intruders?

As the van rounded a bend, and I was about to lose Lorenzo from view, the white snout tilted toward the sky, and another howl echoed into the morning.

I rolled the window down an inch, trying to listen over the rumble of the engine, to hear if there was an answering howl.

Yes, not one but two voices responded with howls from the forested land across the freeway. Soon, the entire pack would know that I'd been out here with the lone wolf who'd attacked my cousins.

19

Drizzle started on the drive back. When we returned to Shoreline, Bolin was waiting outside the leasing office, two coffee cups in hand, one again chilled and topped with whipped cream, the other a hot beverage with steam wafting through the hole in the lid. He also had a thick book with a leather binding tucked under one arm, a placeholder ribbon dangling from its yellowed pages. Did that have to do with the case?

I recalled having it appear in my mind when I'd been a wolf, along with the certainty that I would learn something if I examined it while in that form.

"There you are," Bolin said as I walked up, though Duncan had managed to get me back five minutes before office hours began.

He'd parked his van in a staff spot and watched me head up the walkway. When I looked back, thinking of our interrupted kiss, he lifted his metal detector, as if promising he would be around if I wanted to visit later. My gut flip-flopped with nervous anticipation at the thought of a lunchtime break in his van. He'd said he would leave soon, but we'd had a moment after that, hadn't we? Maybe he would linger longer.

"Here I am." Forcing my attention to Bolin, I pointed at the book. "What's in there?"

"Instructions on how to get rid of fungi."

"Fungi? Did a tenant complain about mushrooms sprouting by their patio?"

"Not mushrooms. The mold you asked me to look into. It's a fungus, remember?"

"Oh right." I couldn't keep the disappointment out of my voice. Even though mold *was* the scourge of the Pacific Northwest, and eradicating it from the complex was always a priority, I'd hoped Bolin had found more information related to the case. "Is there anything about magical remediation in there?"

"There is. I'm still researching, and I'll need to find another spell to retard growth if there are leaks again in the future, but there's an enchantment in here that can eradicate fungi and at least temporarily keep it from coming back. I *think* I know how to place it." Bolin bit his lip. "Hypothetically. I'm a neophyte in this area."

"If it turns out that you can wave your hand, murmur druidic words, and magically deal with mold, I may not let you walk away from this job."

"This job? You mean this unpaid internship that I'm doing so I can learn a good work ethic, gain real-world experience, and prove myself to my parents?" His nose crinkled with distaste, and I had no doubt some of that was a direct quote.

"Maybe I could ask them to pay you." I hadn't wanted an intern, but that had been before I'd believed he could be useful. "And mold is so insidious in Seattle that you could start a lucrative business going around to apartment complexes and applying that magic. I suppose you couldn't *tell* people you were using paranormal remediation means. Maybe you could claim it's a new chemical process."

Bolin leaned against a post for support. "Driving around Seattle to remediate mold is *not* the kind of travel I'm interested in doing."

"St. Lucia might have mold too," I said, plucking out one of the places he'd mentioned where his parents had property.

Bolin gave me an aggrieved look.

I lowered my voice and stepped closer to him. "Do you still have that wolf case at your father's house?"

"Yeah. I got the impression that you didn't want it on the premises here." He glanced toward Duncan's van.

I hadn't told him anything about Duncan's keen interest in it, and certainly hadn't mentioned the cameras, but Bolin was smart enough to figure out more than I'd said. At the least, he knew that such a rare magical artifact had value—he probably knew that better than I.

"Will you bring it back tomorrow?" I asked. "Or tonight would be even better."

With the full moon due that evening, it would be easier for me to change. The day after, I was less certain about.

"Tonight? You want me to drive all the way home and then come *back* here?"

"Yeah, it's called working late. Interns have to do it all the time."

"Fetching a trinket for you isn't in my job description."

"Are you sure? Long ago, when I was an intern, I had to do all sorts of gopher jobs. Well, *go-for* jobs is what I think we called them."

Bolin sighed, looking like he would prefer to be anywhere but here after five p.m.

"Bring it back to me this evening, magically eradicate the mold in that apartment, and I'll tell your parents that you're a fine intern and I've taught you everything they wanted you to learn."

He sighed again. "Do you know what the root of the word *bribery* is?"

"You might not have guessed because of the intelligence gleaming in my eyes, but I don't know the roots of many words."

"Except werewolf." Bolin's eyebrows twitched. "I heard Animal Control swung by because a tenant reported big gray dogs fighting on the lawn. Wolves, she told them, but he put coyotes in his report."

He'd put that in his report because that's what *I'd* told him.

"When you build an apartment complex next to the woods, you might get some wild critters," I said blandly.

"Hm." The way Bolin eyed me made me wonder if he was reassessing his belief in werewolves. He also looked toward Duncan's van again.

I patted him on the shoulder. "If I'm not here when you come back with the case, you can leave it in the office in a drawer, but don't tell anyone about it, okay?"

Especially anyone with a magic detector.

"All right." Coffees in hand, Bolin stepped into the office.

I spotted a tenant with a leashed dog approaching and raised a hand to close the door, not wanting anyone to hear a chance comment about the case. Before I could close it, Bolin leaned out again.

"The medieval word *briber* originally meant trickster, beggar, or robber. The bribes were their ill-gotten gains."

"Fascinating." I closed the door on him.

When the tenant walked up, a curly-haired Doodle mix at her side, I braced myself for a comment about wolves or coyotes. All she did was inform me that the poop-bag dispenser by the dog potty area needed to be refilled. The mundaneness of the request filled me with relief.

As I headed to one of the storage sheds to grab supplies, I attempted to focus on the work issues that needed to be addressed that day, but my thoughts kept wandering. Somewhere along the line, I'd decided that I would indeed go to my family's hunt that night. I needed to learn, as my mother had suggested, what was motivating my cousins to come after me.

After the previous night's hunt, I felt more confident about going out to join the pack. I wasn't confident they would tell me what I wanted to learn, but I doubted I would embarrass myself. I remembered how to change into a wolf and how to *be* a wolf. Over the years, I might have done my best to forget the magic, but the magic hadn't forgotten me.

During the previous night's hunt, I hadn't glimpsed myself in any pools of water, so I hoped I was as *magnificent* as Duncan had claimed. Since the gray in his hair showed up when he was in wolf form, I worried that mine would too, that the pack would see me as old and weak. I'd felt strong and powerful when we'd taken down the deer, but facing an ungulate without fangs wasn't the same as confronting another wolf. And I might have to confront *multiple* wolves.

After filling the bag dispensers on the grounds, I looked toward Duncan's van again. Unfortunately, I couldn't ask him to come along for moral support—the pack would find his presence even more offensive than mine. But I wondered if I should tell him what I planned and ask him for advice. Or would he just listen to me rant about my family? He *had* said he would be available if I wanted to talk.

"Do you want to talk or finish that kiss?" I muttered to myself.

Instead of answering, I headed to the van.

Despite waving his metal detector earlier, I didn't think he'd left with it. Was he taking a nap in his bed? He wasn't visible in the cab, so I assumed he was doing something back there. Maybe his equipment needed lubing.

As I approached, the morning's drizzle turning to rain, his voice drifted out through the window I'd left open earlier.

"You didn't tell me she was so hot," came distinct words from the back.

I froze. Who was he talking to?

"Especially as a wolf," he added with a soft laugh.

He was talking to someone about *me*. Someone who knew I was a *werewolf*? What the hell? That narrowed the possibilities a lot.

A thunk came from inside, like the lid of a case closing.

I lunged to press myself against the side of the van so Duncan wouldn't see me if he looked out a window. Ears straining, I tried to catch the other side of the conversation. My werewolf senses had been improving as more and more days passed since the last dosage of my potion, so maybe...

"You saw her as a wolf?"

Horror, chagrin, anger, and other emotions I couldn't name ran through my body. My hands clenched into fists. I recognized that voice. Chad.

"Yeah," Duncan said. "We hunted together."

"You're not supposed to be *hunting* with her. Or talking to her at all. I didn't hire you to go up there and contemplate her *hotness*."

My jaw clenched as much as my fists. Betrayal entered the mix of emotions tightening my chest and making me want to punch things—starting with Duncan's van.

The bastard who'd cleaned out our savings accounts—including our kids' *college fund*—had paid Duncan to come here? To come and... do what? Spy on me?

"I know. Relax. I found your box, but she was with me at the time, so I couldn't take it."

The wolf case. Of course. Duncan had tried to get me to leave him alone with it.

"Why couldn't you search the apartment when she wasn't there?" Chad asked.

"She's there a lot. She works here, you know."

"No shit, but you're supposed to be an expert at your job."

"I'm an expert at finding things, not breaking into people's apartments and stealing them."

"It's *my* artifact. It's not stealing."

I was so angry that I almost didn't have room to allow confusion into my mangled mix of emotions. But my brain did stutter over that line. Where would Chad have gotten a case made by druids? And why would he have even wanted it?

"It's taking what's rightfully mine," Chad continued, "that *she* kept me from getting when I went back for it."

"You didn't mention where you got it."

I had little doubt that Chad had stolen it and that it wasn't truly his, as he claimed. What right could he have to a druidic artifact?

"That's none of your business. I'm only paying you to retrieve it."

"I did go back to her apartment when she was gone," Duncan said, "but she'd moved it somewhere. I haven't sensed it since we were alone together."

"What do you mean *alone together*? You'd better not be screwing her."

"Why do you care? You left her, right?"

"She's still my wife, you bastard."

I most certainly was *not*. Just because he'd refused to sign the divorce papers didn't mean we were still married in the state of Washington.

"That's not what she said."

"Don't listen to what she says," Chad snapped. "She's not what she pretends to be."

I wished that weren't true.

"Were you the one to put the cameras in her bedroom?" Duncan asked. "To keep an eye on your box? Or on *her*?"

Chad didn't answer the question. Instead, voice so low I barely caught it, he said, "I can't believe she's turning wolf. *Now*. All those years, I wanted to see that. I wanted..."

"To sleep with that?" Duncan asked.

"Hell, yeah, I wanted to see the wolf come out. I could always *feel* her magic, like she was part animal, strong and sexy as hell. Why do you think I kept coming back all those years? I never wanted to be married and chained to a woman."

"Didn't you have children with her?"

"Not intentionally. That was *her* wish."

I ground my teeth at the lie. We'd agreed to have children. He'd said he wanted them too. He'd actually been *around* back in the early years of our marriage.

The revisionist history, and listening to them talk about me, made me seethe. I wanted so badly to leap into the van and strangle Duncan. Even more, I wanted to strangle Chad, but he probably wasn't in the country. He could be calling from his girl-friend's *yacht*. I hoped the same pirates who'd shot Duncan found Chad and filled him with lead.

As the cool rain fell, pattering on my head and running down my flushed cheeks, it crossed my mind to wonder if they'd met on some dock in an exotic locale. World travelers cavorting around and doing who knew what.

"Just get the damn artifact," Chad said. "I've been searching a long time for what's inside."

"What *is* inside? Knowing might help me guess where she would have put it."

"That's none of your business either. Force her to tell you where it is if you can't find it on your own."

"I'm not forcing a woman to do anything."

"Finding things is supposed to be your great expertise."

"It is. I'll keep looking around. I don't know why you couldn't get it yourself though. You put it in that heat duct, didn't you?"

"Years ago. Before I'd figured out how to open it. And before she put out a restraining order on me. I *tried* to go back for it, but she's turned into a real bitch."

"Since she found out you were screwing other women?"

"Don't sound so sanctimonious. You were flirting with one of *my* girls right in front of me."

"She was flirting with *me*."

"Fuck off, wolf."

"That's no way to talk to someone doing you a favor."

"You're charging me a fortune to collect something that's rightfully mine," Chad said. "It's practically extortion."

"This was *your* idea."

"Just get the damn case. I wouldn't have left it if I thought she was going to change the locks and would physically throw me out when I showed up. I thought having it under a werewolf's bed, however diminished a wolf she always was when I knew her, would be safer than sticking it in a bank vault, but that was a mistake."

"I'm guessing you've made a lot of them."

"Fuck off," Chad repeated and hung up.

"He really inspires loyalty in the people he hires," Duncan muttered.

Unable to contain my anger any longer, I threw open his sliding door and glared into the van.

Duncan fumbled the phone and almost dropped it.

"You were *hired* to come here and search my apartment and steal something?" I demanded. "And you had the gall to *flirt* with me? To *kiss* me? When you were working for the one person in the world I truly loathe?"

"Well, if the case belongs to him—"

"*Belongs* to him? A priceless, centuries-old magical artifact made with druid magic? How the *hell* would Chad have become the rightful owner of something like that?"

"Druid magic?"

"He had to have stolen it," I roared, ignoring the question. "There was no way my idiot, conniving, and entirely magicless mundane husband got it legitimately. He hasn't done anything *legitimately* in his whole life."

"I suppose that's possible." Duncan looked flustered for the first time since I'd met him. "But you didn't know it was there, so—"

"So it was okay for you to barge into my apartment with your *magic detector* to find it and take it?"

My voice had risen to a yell. Maybe a scream. A couple of people who'd been heading from their cars to their apartments paused to watch us.

Maybe I should have toned it down, but, in that moment, I was too furious to do so. Furious that Duncan had betrayed me. Furious that Chad was still in my life after betraying me over and over again. Furious that my cousin was trying to kill me. Furious about *everything*.

The rage flowing through my veins made my nerves tingle and my skin prickle with heat. Hell, was I going to change in the parking lot in the middle of the day?

No. I wanted to punch Duncan—I wanted to shift into a wolf and rip his throat out—but I made myself step back. Voice hoarse, I said, "Get out of my parking lot."

Duncan lifted his hands. "Look, I'm sorry, Luna. I just came here to find a lost thing. It sounded like an adventure, and you understand that I crave that, right? I didn't mean to—"

"Get out!" I thrust a finger toward the exit. "Or I'll have your van towed and dumped into Puget Sound, and you'll never find a magnet big enough to lift it out. Especially since I'm going to kick your ass all the way to Canada while that's happening."

Duncan opened his mouth again, but I growled. It came from deep within my chest and sounded far more like a wolf growl than anything a human could utter.

He must have realized how close I was to changing and making good on my threats.

"Okay." Duncan fished in his pocket and flicked something toward me, like someone tossing a coin into a fountain.

Worried it was more dangerous than a *coin*, I jumped back instead of catching it. The small object landed on the pavement with a faint *tink*.

My wariness made Duncan shake his head sadly, but all he did was whisper, "Good luck," before closing the sliding door, climbing into the cab, and starting the van.

My chest rose and fell with deep breaths. I couldn't stop seething. Even more people had stopped to watch, and I tried to calm myself. I couldn't change into a werewolf in front of them. I'd lose my job if I did. I might lose everything.

I snatched up the small coin—no, it was the locket we'd found the night before—and almost hurled it after Duncan, but that wouldn't do anything. Besides, his van was already rumbling through puddles on its way out, spraying the mailboxes at the entrance. It turned out into the street and drove away.

I stood there for a long time, my fists clenched and rain falling on my head.

20

I EYED THE FUEL GAUGE ON THE DASHBOARD AS MY TRUCK RUMBLED through Monroe and into the woods for the second time that week. Since I lived and worked in the same place, I didn't usually drive much—or budget much for fuel. The amount of cash left in the GAS envelope wouldn't fill the tank. My life had grown very odd this week.

"Tonight, we resolve this. One way or another."

Except that I could only hope to resolve *part* of my problem. There was still that case.

I'd hoped Bolin would return with it before I left, but he'd texted that he needed to wait for his father to get home to open the safe. I appreciated that it was being stored in a good place, but I'd hoped I might be able to take a look at it through wolf eyes before leaving to meet my family. Maybe I could have learned something new about it, something that might have given me an advantage if I had to deal with pack members who didn't want me to survive tonight's hunt.

Since I hadn't told my mother for certain that I was coming, I hoped my cousins wouldn't have time to plan anything. A part of me wished they wouldn't be there at all, but they were the reason I was going. They were the ones I needed answers from.

"One way or another," I repeated softly.

Tonight, clouds hid the moon, but I could still feel the call of its magic as I approached the long driveway that led to my mother's cabin. Before turning in, I stopped the truck and dug into my pocket, pulling out the locket that I'd almost hurled back at Duncan. Instead, as I'd seen the witch do in the vision, I grasped it and tilted my face toward the night sky in the direction of the moon. Because of the clouds, I couldn't see it with my eyes, but I sensed its presence. Always.

A faint charge of magic swept through me, making my insides buzz and gooseflesh rise on my arms. For a moment, I felt amazing —almost *invincible*. But all too soon, the sensation faded, and I questioned whether the locket had done anything.

I hadn't wanted to come up here to hunt with my cousins without a plan, but I hadn't been able to think of much. Other than the locket, it wasn't as if I had a stash of magical artifacts that could protect me. Nor could I have packed guns under a trench coat. As I'd learned long ago, clothing and items disappeared into the ether during a werewolf change. If I wanted to shoot my cousins, it would have to be as a human, and then... Then I'd have to worry about more than the family's ire. What happened as a wolf tended not to be punishable by human laws, since they didn't acknowledge that our kind existed. But in the world of humans... things were different. Repercussions were different.

Sighing, I put the locket away, hoping the magic had done *something*. I also hoped I wouldn't need it, that the hunt would go better than expected.

"Wishful thinking."

I drove up the driveway, the window cracked, allowing in the night scent. It had stopped raining, but the air still smelled of damp foliage and earth. It was invigorating and, under different circumstances, I might have looked forward to this.

When I reached the cabin, wolves who'd already changed were meandering through the area, and men and a couple of women lounged on the porch. All sets of eyes, lupine and human, turned toward my truck. My memory dredged up names for faces I hadn't seen in more than twenty years. Some of the younger faces I'd never seen.

When I spotted Augustus, I had to resist the urge to turn the truck around and hit the accelerator. As I reminded myself, he was the one I needed answers from. Hopefully, the presence of the rest of the family would force him to be civil—or at least not attack me without provocation. But it was hard to be certain of that, especially when I thought the young man next to him on the porch, his elbows propped on the railing, was one of the people—the then *wolf*—who'd helped attack Duncan.

Given recent revelations, I felt less guilty now about my family attacking Duncan. I almost wondered if they'd known he was up to no good. That didn't, however, explain Augustus trying to kill *me*.

There was no sign of my mother, not yet. The lights weren't on in the cabin. Did she intend to hunt with us? She was the only one I could be fairly certain wasn't plotting against me.

I parked next to a couple of trucks, no doubt belonging to other pack members who lived in the city most of the time and came out for hunts. When I turned mine off, I had to wipe my palms on my sweatpants before getting out. The idea of undressing in front of this crowd didn't appeal, but some of the men on the porch were already removing their clothes as they glanced toward the cloudy sky.

The young and affable Emilio trotted down the steps to the driveway, waving for another man to follow him, one who looked similar aside from a shorter haircut and less baby fat on the face. An older brother?

"Hi, Luna. Glad you could come." Emilio lifted a hand in a wave, or maybe to pat me on the shoulder, but it diverted toward the passenger door of my truck. Grinning, he opened it and sniffed the interior. "Did you bring any more giant salamis? That was amazing, but my brother and his wife stole most of it."

"We just wanted a *piece* of it." The older sibling held up thumb and forefinger to demonstrate the size of the piece.

Emilio shook his head and held out his arms to demonstrate a piece larger than the original salami had been. "You can't use wolf fangs to bite off a *piece*. You took *most* of it."

"I had to. Tanya is trying to get pregnant. She needs nourishment. Also, she's huge as a wolf and can kick my ass if I don't treat her right."

"*Most* people can kick your ass," Augustus grumbled from the porch, watching our exchange through narrowed eyes.

"I did bring some summer sausages." I delved into the seat well to hold up a large gift box that had done even more to deplete my budget this month than the need for extra gas. Next pay period, I might have to start an envelope labeled WEREWOLF BRIBES. "Enough for everyone who wants some." I eyed Augustus. "Even those who don't deserve gifts."

His lip curled in a sneer—or maybe a *snarl*.

"Perfect!" Oblivious to our glares, Emilio grabbed the gift box. "I'll dole out the sausage fairly."

"Sure you will." His brother peered over his shoulder as Emilio opened the box.

A couple more men walked off the porch to investigate its contents. Several wolves with nostrils twitching in the air also wandered over.

At least *some* of the family might think more kindly of me if I brought gifts every time I visited.

Augustus jumped off the porch, shoulder muscles flexing against the fabric of a black T-shirt, and walked toward me. I tensed and, for a fleeting moment, wished Duncan were there, standing at my side to face my cousin. But no, I couldn't wish for that. Duncan's betrayal stung me even more than that of my cousin. He'd accepted a job from my loathsome ex. Augustus was only trying to kill me. Maybe it wasn't logical, but that seemed like a lesser crime.

My cousin stopped in front of me, looking me slowly up and down.

"You've heeded the call," he stated.

I almost asked how he knew but remembered the white wolf who'd spotted us before dawn and had shared the word—the howl—of our hunt. By now, the whole pack probably knew. It was also possible that Augustus could smell or magically sense the change in me.

"Yeah," I admitted.

Augustus lifted his arm, and I tensed, prepared to spring away. My blood heated, tingling in my veins, the wolf ready to be unleashed.

But Augustus thumped me on the shoulder. "Good. It's about time. Your mom is relieved."

He looked and pointed toward the front of the cabin.

I eyed his profile. Did his words mean he wasn't after me anymore? I couldn't believe that my use of the potion and refusal to change had been the only reasons he'd attacked in the first place.

"Can we talk for a few minutes, Augustus?" I asked.

Maybe I could learn what I needed without going off on a hunt with him.

The front door opened before he replied, and the white wolf I'd seen the night before padded out of the cabin. Lorenzo. My mom, still in her human form, came out after him. Her shirt was half unbuttoned. I didn't know if that meant she'd just had sex—did seventy-year-old women with cancer still feel the *urge* to have sex?—or simply that she was prepared to change and hunt with us. The latter seemed more likely. *That*, I trusted, werewolves would do until the day they died.

"Later," Augustus replied and walked away, tugging his T-shirt over his head. Recent wounds marred his back, the blows that Duncan had landed on him.

As more people tugged off their clothes, tossing them on trucks and the porch railing, a woman in her late twenties walked over. She glanced toward the guys—and wolves—delving into the sausage box, and I thought that might have been what brought her over, but she stopped in front of me. Wearing a UW hoodie and with her black hair swept back into a perky ponytail, she looked like a college student.

"Hi, Luna. Do you remember me?"

"Uhm, sorry, I don't."

"This might help." With a self-deprecating smirk, she stuck her phone out, tapped the photos app, and held up a picture of a black-haired toddler wandering around with pudgy legs, as revealed by a lack of pants. "My mom posted that on Facebook recently to mortify me and use my kindness against me—*I* was the one who scanned her old photo albums so she would have digital copies. Anyway, that's probably about how I looked the last time we met."

"Jasmine?" I guessed.

"Your niece, yup."

"I thought my half-sister—your mom—and her husband left the pack to return to the Old World. That's what I heard."

"Oh, they did. Back in the day." Jasmine waved dismissively. "But they've been back for ages, and I finished school here. There are more wild mountains and forested lands left here, and they liked the hunting better. Also, there were job opportunities for

software engineers. Dad's a big geek and works in game develop-
ment in Redmond."

"A geeky werewolf sounds great."

"Mom thinks so." Jasmine winked. "She's a real-estate agent
now and kind of knows about you because you work for the
Sylvans. She's kept tabs on you for your mom. We almost went
over to see you a couple of times but weren't sure... Well, nobody
was sure if you wanted to see the pack."

"I didn't think the pack wanted to see *me*."

Wistfulness filled me. After my cousin's attempts on my life, it
was hard to feel that my instincts had been wrong, but I wished I
had known at least some of the pack didn't resent me, that we
could have stayed in touch. In light of Mom's illness, I especially
wished I hadn't waited so long to check in on her. But would the
family have let me get close?

I glanced at Augustus, but he was naked now and down on all
fours, on the brink of changing. I looked away.

"Some care more about people's choices than others." Jasmine
waved again. "*Some* know we need all the help we can get to
ensure the pack—*all* packs—survive into the future."

"Yes," I said.

My conversation with my mother came to mind, her bringing
up the loss of the ability to spread the wolf magic through bite and
how our kind were dwindling.

"I need to talk to you about something when we get a minute."
Jasmine glanced toward the sky, as if the moon were an hourglass,
sand ticking down until we all had to change. In a way, it was. I
could feel it compelling me, calling to the wolf. Maybe she did too.
"It's about—"

A growl came from the trees beside the driveway, and Jasmine
stopped.

Emilio hadn't changed yet, but he was engaged in tug-of-war
with a wolf who had. He had the gift box tucked under one arm

while he gripped a foot-long sausage with the other. The wolf had its fangs sunk into the other end, growling as it tried to pull the prize free. They were *both* growling.

"I *said* I'd divvy it up," Emilio said. "With a *knife*. You can't just tear it in half and take off with that much. You're an *animal*."

"You'd think they didn't have the ability to go to Walmart in human form and buy their own sausage logs," Jasmine said with an eye roll.

"I got the gift boxes from a farm store," I said. "Grass-fed meat without preservatives, so they're probably a lot more appealing than the typical grocery offerings."

"Probably? You're not sure?"

"I didn't buy any for myself." A touch of embarrassment warmed my cheeks, and I didn't confess that I couldn't afford to purchase expensive stuff, not for myself, except maybe for a special occasion.

"Because you don't crave good meat? Or because...?" Jasmine gestured vaguely at me. Apparently, my niece's family keeping tabs on me meant she also knew about the potion. I sighed, wishing that had remained a secret.

"I crave it. Also rich dark chocolate and fancy espresso made from high-quality beans. It's tough maintaining a budget when you have expensive tastes."

Jasmine laughed. "Tell me about it."

The friendly laugh made me relax an iota. Maybe there was hope of reestablishing a relationship with my family. But would I have to stop taking the potion permanently for them to accept me? I doubted the pack would welcome a mundane human who'd forsaken the way of the wolf. There was, after all, a reason we hadn't spoken in so long.

I didn't know if I *could* stop taking the potion. What if I lost it as a wolf and killed again? Someone innocent who didn't deserve such a fate? Even after all this time, the past haunted me.

Another growl came from the side. Emilio fell on his backside as the wolf won the tug-of-war and took off with the entire sausage.

Emilio didn't land hard and rolled to his feet quickly, showing easy athleticism, but it didn't matter. The wolf was already gone.

"Looks like Benito already had a successful hunt for the night," came my mother's dry voice from the porch.

Though the words seemed to be for everyone, she gazed over at me. Most of the pack had changed, and more than a dozen wolves also gazed at me.

My anxiety and damp palms returned. The night before, I'd changed successfully and had no trouble hunting, no pain in my joints or limbs to indicate my advancing age. But what if I couldn't do the same tonight? When it mattered?

Mom removed her clothes, draping them over the railing with others.

"Time to go." Jasmine stepped back to do the same. "We can talk after. Don't go home right away, okay? It's important."

"Okay."

I would have liked to learn whatever she had to say *before* the hunt. Might she be a resource who knew what had prompted Augustus to turn into an asshole?

But, after tossing her clothes on the hood of my truck, Jasmine stepped away.

My phone vibrated in my pocket. I almost ignored it, but I'd been waiting for a text from Bolin, and it was his name that popped up on the screen, the message slipping in on the one bar of cell signal.

Uhm, I lost the case, Luna. A big burly guy with some magic about him jumped out at me when I got to the apartments. He beat me up and stole it. I'm at the ER getting stitches.

I stared in horror, distressed that Bolin had been hurt—from the description, the aggressor could have been another werewolf

—and dismayed that he'd lost the case. Even though it had never been mine, I'd hoped... Well, I didn't know. That it could help me with the pack, I guess.

When I dialed Bolin to apologize for the attack and make sure he would be all right, the signal wasn't strong enough for the call to go through. I tried texting, but the phone informed me that the message couldn't be sent. I bared my teeth at the screen.

Augustus, in his wolf form, padded past. I glared, more determined than ever to get answers from him.

A few feet away, Jasmine threw her head back, a lupine howl coming from her throat as the change took her. Other werewolves who'd already turned also threw their heads back and howled at the sky.

The clouds parted enough to allow a silver beam of light through. It gleamed on the hoods of vehicles and in the eyes of the wolves.

A surge of power swept through me, the moon magic demanding that I change, demanding I let the wolf come forth to hunt. The magic was so intense that I barely got my phone put away and my clothes off before the change took me.

Soon, I stood on all fours in the driveway. My mother and the big white wolf led the way into the woods, and the pack fanned out behind them.

More howls serenaded the night. The hunt had begun.

21

As a wolf, my instincts drove me, and my human memories and concerns grew hazy. I forgot about Duncan's betrayal, the stolen case, and the treachery of my cousin, and loped through the forest with the pack, moonlight brightening the way. As a wolf inhaling the night's scents and hearing every sound in the forest around us, all I could think about was the joy of the hunt and the overriding desire to find game.

And find it, we did. We swept into the foothills of the mountains, with dense evergreens rising around us and a river cutting through the forest, its roar drawing us. We came upon elk bedded down for the night and startled them into flight. With so many wolves, we were unmatchable. We were the supreme predators of the land, and we took down our prey and ate our fill.

I caught a dark-gray wolf—Augustus—watching me and remembered to be wary of him, but when he tilted his head back to howl his satisfaction at the successful kill, I did the same. We all did. The night sang to us, demanding we acknowledge the magic that nature had granted us.

After finishing the elk, the pack took a circuitous route

through their territory, checking for intruders and enjoying the magic of the moon. We loped easily along the riverbanks, some pausing to lap up the cool refreshing water. Our powerful muscles carried us over boulders and down inclines as the waterway grew frothy. It headed downhill and gained width and depth as streams flowed into it.

A hint of a musky scent rose over the damp vegetation growing along the river. A moose had come this way. It was a rare find in this part of the state, and joy filled me at the contemplation of battling such strong prey.

Half the pack splashed through the river to run on the other side, seeking the moose's trail there. Guided by instincts that believed it had remained on the closer side, I stayed there, following the waterway downstream. Soon, though, the terrain grew more difficult to navigate, the riverbanks turning into steep canyon walls.

The scent of game propelled us onward, led by—

My step faltered as I realized Augustus was leading me now. My mother and the white wolf had crossed to the other side. I glimpsed them in the foliage over there, but the river had grown too wide and treacherous to follow them over. Jasmine and Emilio had ended up over there too. None of the wolves who'd been friendly to me were on this side, but some more of my cousins were.

My hackles rose with the certainty that trouble was coming. Oh, it was possible this was all accidental, that we would simply hunt together and nothing would happen, but I doubted it. My lupine instincts had been so preoccupied by the hunt that I'd allowed myself to be singled out, to be surrounded by werewolves who'd already tried to kill me.

Ahead, the moonlight shone on a railroad trestle bridge that crossed high over the river. There. That was my chance to get to the other side, to where the rest of the family hunted.

Hoping to gain the lead so my cousins couldn't mess with me, I pumped my legs, bounding along the rocky rim of a canyon. The river roared through it far below, much wider and faster than it had been miles upstream.

The moonlight brightening the bridge showed wide railroad ties that offered sturdy purchase, but, as I ran out on it, I couldn't help but glance down at the frothing water visible below. *Far below.*

A questioning howl came from the forest on the other side. It was my mother's voice, and it sounded like she'd traveled away from the river. Or... been *led* away from the river? It might have been my imagination, but I thought I caught a hint of concern in her howl.

I parted my jaws, intending to send an answering call so she would know where I was, but two huge wolves trotted onto the trestle from the far side. Paws on the wooden ties, they sank low, setting themselves as their eyes bored into me.

My gut twisted, and I slowed down. They were there to block me—or worse.

When I glanced back, the dark-gray wolf that was Augustus padded onto the bridge from the other side. Another cousin came up beside him, the wolf with the black-tipped tail who'd helped attack Duncan.

Damn it. They'd led me to this. I'd walked into their trap.

One-on-one, I might have held my own against any of them, but I didn't like the odds of winning a fight against two of them. Or, if I couldn't handle the situation quickly enough, against all *four* of them.

Even as I debated what to do, the two wolves in front trotted out onto the trestle toward me. The wolves behind me closed from that direction.

I glanced over the edge at the water roaring past below. It was hard to tell how deep it was, but that froth made me suspect boulders down there might kill me if I fell.

Farther downstream, a pool of darker and quieter water didn't appear as treacherous. If I jumped, I might be able to reach that spot, to land without hitting rocks.

But something told me these guys *wanted* me to do that. And that it wouldn't be good for my health.

It would be better to knock *them* into the water.

Since the wolves coming from the far side blocked the way to my mother and the part of the pack that might help, they were the logical ones to attack. But Augustus had started all this. For whatever reason, he'd made himself my enemy. This was *his* plan. I had no doubt.

I snarled at the approaching wolves, then turned sideways and crouched, as if I would leap from the bridge. All four wolves picked up their speed, running toward me, intending to knock me off if I didn't jump.

At the last moment, I whirled toward Augustus and charged between him and his ally. Surprise flickered in their eyes, but they braced themselves, and their jaws opened, ready to attack.

There was no way I wouldn't be hurt. Knowing that, I still rushed in, lunging for Augustus's throat. At the same time, I swung my hips toward his ally, hoping to knock one or both wolves off the bridge. It wasn't that wide.

Augustus was ready and met my snapping jaws in a bite of his own. I knocked his snout aside with my own, like a sword fighter parrying an attack, and rammed my shoulder into his as I intentionally bumped the other wolf. He sank his fangs into my hindquarters, but I was so focused on Augustus that I hardly cared. Magic and adrenaline surging through my veins made me fast. Before Augustus could bring his jaws back to me, I bit into his flesh. He shifted enough to keep me from tearing into his throat, but my fangs sank deep between his shoulder and neck, and he cried out.

The metallic tang of blood washed over my tongue. Snarls and pants filled the air, audible over the roar of the river.

Holding on so that he couldn't maneuver, I surged forward, ignoring the fiery pain that ignited in my back from the other wolf's bite. With all the power in my limbs and torso, I pushed against Augustus. As he attempted to shake me off and escape, one of his paws slipped off the trestle. He lunged to keep his balance, trying to stay on the bridge, but I shoved him without mercy. Only when he lurched fully over the edge did I let go of him.

I spun toward his ally. The other wolf had released me but only so he could bite again, higher along my flank. He was trying to work his way to my neck. These roadkill lickers all wanted me dead.

Furious and indignant, I lunged and bit him three times so quickly it stunned him. Hot blood ran down my leg from my wounds, but I didn't care. I barely felt the pain over the rage filling me, the instinct to kill that charged through my wolf blood, threatening to take over my rational mind.

As I bit in for the fourth time, tearing a chunk out of the side of my foe's neck, he flung himself backward. He went over the opposite side of the trestle, pitching toward the frothing water below.

Before I could turn or plan another move, something slammed into me from behind. The other two wolves had reached me.

I whirled, biting, but they didn't want to engage in a fang fight. Accepting my bites, they used their shoulders and chests to shove at me.

Alone, I might have braced myself and pushed back, but their combined power was too much for me. Worse, my paw came down on a tie slick with algae. I tried to get better footing, but they succeeded in shoving me off, just as I'd done to Augustus.

As damp cold air whistled past me, I looked toward the moon watching from high above. This might be my end, but at least I'd stood up for myself. And I'd died a wolf. So be it.

22

I LANDED IN THE ICY WATER, THE COLD SHOCKING ME AS MY WOUNDS burned from the contact. Gravity plunged me to the bottom of the river, and I'd barely slowed when I struck a submerged boulder. New pain erupted at the jarring blow, and my air escaped my lungs. The river swept me downstream with startling ferocity, spinning me about until I couldn't tell up from down.

Though I pawed at the water, trying to swim to a calmer spot or at least find air, I couldn't make progress against the whirling current. I clipped another boulder and lashed out in frustration, snapping at the water.

A boom cracked from nearby. What the— Was that a gunshot?

Finally, I flowed into calmer water, the pool I'd noticed before, and managed to get my snout to the surface. My paws brushed against the pebble-covered river bottom. I longed to surge onto solid land, but the gunshot made me hesitate to crawl out. Staying low, I peered toward shore.

On a rocky ledge overlooking the river, two camo-wearing men pointed rifles. I tensed, but they weren't facing me. Their firearms angled skyward, upriver and toward the bridge. The water had carried me thirty or forty yards downstream, but the trestle remained visible, silhouetted against the night sky. Two wolves on it were *also* silhouetted.

My first thought was that the hunters were aiming at my cousin's thuggish allies, and I started to wish the men good luck. But wait. That was a white wolf up there. And a silver female wolf. My mother and Lorenzo. They must have come out of the woods and onto the railroad trestle to look for me. Now, with a gunshot fired, they were running toward cover.

"Get them this time," one man blurted.

"I will," the other said, finger tightening on the trigger of his rifle.

I snarled and surged out of the water toward the hunters.

As had happened so long ago, my wolf instincts took over completely. The wild rage of a hurt animal, an *angry* animal, drove all rational thought out of my mind. I barely felt the pain from my wounds as I sprinted at the hunters. All I knew was that I had to keep them from killing my mother, from hurting the pack.

The men heard my splashes as I raced out of the water and paused.

"Look out for that one!" One hunter swung his rifle toward me.

"That message wasn't kidding." The other man pointed in my direction. "Wolves are all over."

I dove sideways as they fired. One bullet ricochetted off the rocky bank. One grazed my shoulder, fiery pain blasting me.

They swore and took aim again, but, by then, I'd reached them. With nothing but werewolf instincts and savagery guiding me, I tore into them.

My last conscious thought before my awareness disappeared into a red and black haze was that it was happening again. It was like it had been all those years ago when I'd killed Raoul. I couldn't stop the magic and wildness that took me over the edge. I bit and snarled and knocked my targets down, driven by fury, driven by the instincts and intense power of the werewolf.

That magical imperative didn't wane until the hunters lay dead, their rifles fallen near their bodies.

Awareness returned slowly, as my ragged panting sounded in my ears, and water and blood dripped onto the rocky bank under my paws. My numerous wounds tingled with warmth as much as pain, some unfamiliar magic affecting them. Healing them? The tingling wasn't something I'd experienced before, so maybe it had to do with that locket. I didn't know, but I was on my feet when I probably shouldn't have been. And I had the strength to turn and look for more threats as my rational mind returned, along with the awareness that my cousin had laid this trap. I had no doubt that he had told these hunters that wolves would be available to bag tonight in this spot. He and his allies had intentionally driven me in this direction.

On my side of the river but downstream, the dark-gray wolf that was Augustus limped into view, wet and glaring at me. I snarled, ready to rip his throat out. *Wanting* to rip his throat out.

Emilio padded out of the woods and onto the rock ledge, not far from me. Jasmine and several others followed. Finally, my mother and Lorenzo came out of the trees, her pelt even more silver under the moonlight. Fortunately, she didn't appear wounded. Neither of them did.

Uncertainty trickled into me, displacing the rage. Or maybe it was simply that my battle lust was fading.

Mom stopped, sitting on her haunches, and gazed at the dead men. Later, I would feel regret for allowing the savagery of the werewolf magic to take me over, to turn me into a crazed monster. I had been defending myself and my mother, but it was too similar to when I'd lost Raoul.

As my fury waned, the magic did too. I'd answered the call of the wolf, and that was done for now. I changed back into my human form, as did some of the others. With the absence of fur, the chill autumn air was biting, but I didn't shy away from it. In my human form, the memory of all that I'd longed to learn returned to me. It was time to get some answers.

"My daughter," Mom said, having also changed. "You have returned to us."

I grimaced and glanced at the bodies. There probably wouldn't be ramifications when the authorities found them, since their wounds proclaimed they'd been killed by a wild animal, and the law didn't acknowledge the existence of *werewolves*, but I couldn't help but worry and feel that I'd been forced into this. To kill. Again.

"Were you part of setting this up?" I didn't think she had been, but... I had to ask. I had to *know*.

"Not I." Mom frowned sternly toward Augustus.

His battle lust must have also cooled, because he slumped against a tree in his human form, chest abraded and bleeding from the fall.

"Come here, Augustus," Mom called. "I will hear your explanation, or I will ask you to leave the pack."

Scowling, he looked into the woods behind him, as if he was considering leaving of his own accord. But, ultimately, he walked up the bank toward us. The rest of the pack, some still in wolf form, stood or sat on their haunches to watch.

Augustus stopped several paces away. "You said you were going to leave the wolf medallion to your daughter. Even though she rejected our pack and our kind. Until this night, she kept mutilating herself with magic so she wouldn't turn into a werewolf anymore."

"I'm aware," my mother said coolly. "But when I tested others, including your mate, nobody else caused the artifact to react with acceptance. Even with her power dulled, the medallion desired her touch above all others who gripped it."

I rocked back, feeling dense. Mom had told me about that testing and that Augustus's mate had been in consideration for inheriting the artifact. But I hadn't realized it was so valuable, so important, that it would prompt someone to kill for it. Augustus must have resented me already. For a long time.

"It glowed *some* for my mate," he said.

"Little. It glowed more for my daughter."

"*She* rejected us." Augustus pointed a finger at me. "What does it matter?"

"Once, she did leave us, yes," Mom said. "For reasons that made sense to her at the time. But now... Now she is here. I knew she would return."

I swallowed. I hadn't decided to do that. All this had been about figuring out why Augustus wanted me dead. That was it.

Well, maybe that wasn't true. Since I'd learned Mom was dying... That had changed something too, hadn't it?

"She *wasn't* going to return to us," Augustus said. "It wasn't until I— Until this week, she wanted nothing to do with us."

"Until you *attacked* her," my mother said. "That was what you meant to say, yes?"

He stared at the ground. "Yes."

"She did not challenge you."

"No, she was a puny human who couldn't challenge *anyone*."

I bristled and almost waved to the dead hunters, but slaying people, especially in a fit of animalistic rage, wasn't anything to be proud of. I resented that my cousin had set this up. That a bunch of my family members had been in on it.

"The only reason she came here was to cry to you that the pack wasn't treating her well." Augustus pointed at me again, his finger accusing.

"I came because I wanted to know why you were trying to kill me," I said. "I didn't care about *treatment* in general."

"Whatever brought her," my mother said, glancing toward

Jasmine, "does not matter. Luna is here. She has returned to us." Mom lifted her chin and met my eyes. "*She* is my heir. And you will not attempt to harm her again unless she challenges you for your position in the pack."

Jaw clenched, Augustus didn't answer.

"Did you steal the case from my apartment complex?" I asked Augustus, hoping he would continue to answer and speak the truth with my mother watching. "Or tell someone to do it?" I realized he couldn't have been there, attacking Bolin, at the same time he was at Mom's cabin, getting ready for the hunt.

Augustus glanced at Mom. "I have no idea what you're talking about."

"Case?" Mom asked, watching us both.

"A magical artifact with a toothy wolf on it."

"I'm not familiar with any such artifacts in the area that would have significance to the pack."

I was about to say that it'd been made with druid magic and might not have anything to do with werewolves, but I grew aware of all the eyes watching the conversation, not all of them friendly. Maybe I would talk to my mother about it in private later. It was hard to read through Augustus's surliness whether he had been responsible for the theft or not. *Duncan* was the one who'd been trying to get it all along. Bolin would have recognized him if he'd been the attacker, but it was possible *he'd* hired someone to help.

The tingling in my wounds had worn off. They didn't seem to be bleeding, but weariness settled into me, and I didn't have the strength to ask any more questions. All I wanted was to return home and curl up in bed and sleep for days.

The white wolf, Lorenzo, had stayed back during the discussion, allowing my mother to handle it, but he stepped forward now. With the moon shining on his back, he shifted, morphing into a man I hadn't seen in a long time. He was younger than Mom but not by much, his white hair thick and straight, but his skin weathered and creased. His body was still lean and muscular. Powerful. He stood at Mom's side to face my cousin.

"If you attack my mate's daughter again," Lorenzo told Augustus in a gravelly voice, "you will answer to me."

"And no matter what happens," Mom said, "after this, neither you nor your mate will inherit anything from me. Certainly not that medallion and the hope for our people's future survival."

After giving me a dark look, one that promised he wasn't done with me, Augustus stalked into the woods. Several others took off after him, those who were his allies, those who'd been willing to help him end my life.

I licked dry lips, distressed that I might not have resolved anything tonight.

"I am glad you have returned, my daughter." Mom nodded at me before she and Lorenzo took their wolf forms again to leave.

I pushed my hand through hair wet from my soak in the river and wondered if I could so easily command the wolf to return. After a change and a hunt, the insatiable urge to do so usually faded until a threat or another full moon bestirred my wild instincts again.

Before I could test my abilities, Jasmine walked up. "Are you okay?"

"Bruised. Battered." I glanced at the dead hunters but quickly looked away. "And rattled."

"I would be too. I've never been forced to..." Jasmine waved at the bodies.

"Yeah." I appreciated that she'd used the words *been forced to* for me. I hadn't wanted this. She understood.

"I need to make a confession." Jasmine looked around, but the rest of our kin were leaving, most as wolves, but a few as people, perhaps not able to summon the magic to change again.

I recalled the look my mother had given to Jasmine and nodded. "Go ahead."

"I heard about you being Aunt Umbra's heir and her wanting you to have the medallion and her cabin. She actually called me in along with some of the other female werewolves with reasonable power and strong ties to the pack. She wanted us all to touch the medallion." Jasmine's mouth twisted. "It didn't so much as glow or pulse for me."

"Sorry." It might have been better for my life if it *hadn't* reacted to me in any way. Would it be wrong for me to be envious of my niece?

"I overheard some discussions I wasn't supposed to, such as that Augustus might want to get rid of you to ensure his mate was chosen as the heir. I think he was researching that medallion and knows more about it, maybe even more than your mom. Anyway, I thought about going to warn you, but I knew you weren't... uhm, quite yourself."

She'd known about the potion, yes. She'd already admitted that.

"I dragged my sister to Shoreline, and we... convinced the alchemist lady in your apartment complex to return to her native land. She was from Ireland, did you know?"

"You *convinced* her?"

"Well, we strongly suggested that it was time for her to leave the area. We didn't threaten her, but we did change in front of her, and that might have scared her. She left, which was what we were hoping for."

"Why?"

"So she wouldn't continue to make you potions. So you'd have to come back to us—to your *mother*. Your mom believed it would happen without intervention, that you'd see the light—the *moon*light—and eventually come, but it had been more than twenty-five years, and she was dying... so... we felt we needed to help her. And to help *you*. If Augustus was going to come gunning for you, you needed your wolf power." Jasmine shrugged.

Maybe I should have been mad at the manipulation—and certainly that they'd scared an old lady away—but at least Jasmine had been looking out for my mother. And, I supposed, for me. If I hadn't been out of potions, would I have had a chance of surviving Augustus's attempts to kill me?

Maybe not.

"Beatrice is okay?" I asked.

"She should be. We didn't hurt her. I think she just moved."

"In a hurry. Without leaving her key, collecting her damage deposit, and notifying the leasing office."

"Well, a wolf did growl at her right outside her front door." Jasmine touched her chest. "That can hasten move-outs."

I rubbed my face but didn't contemplate the situation for long. Naked and damp, with the cold night air nipping at my bare skin, I was ready to go home. And I needed to check on Bolin too.

"I should have talked to you about the situation," Jasmine said in an apologetic tone, "but I didn't know you or how you would react or if you hated the pack. None of us have been real sure about you."

"I haven't been real sure about myself either." I'd always thought I would have my whole life figured out by this age, but it seemed more chaotic than ever.

Jasmine smiled uncertainly. "Maybe the witch lady will come back or call when she's recovered from..."

"Being scared off her ass by a giant wolf?"

"It wasn't a *giant* wolf. Just a medium-sized one."

I sighed. "I don't know whether to thank you for wanting to help me or resent you for meddling and terrifying one of my tenants."

"If you decide on the former, I like sausage logs."

"What if I decide on the latter?"

"You can club me with a sausage log?"

"As long as I leave it on the ground for you after I'm done?"

Her smile grew a little braver. "Ideally, yes."

EPILOGUE

As morning settled over Shoreline, I drove into the parking lot for the apartment complex. Since I hadn't been able to summon the wolf again, it had been a long walk back to my mother's cabin and my truck. The sun had come up before I'd made it out of Monroe, my body aching and weary.

I scanned the lot for Duncan's van, and it wasn't there. That should have given me relief, but a touch of wistfulness crept over me. He'd been... entertaining. More, he'd understood the werewolf thing, and he'd been decent company. Too bad my first impression of him had been right, that his arrival here had been suspicious. In the end, I'd been foolish to let my guard down.

Yawning, I parked in a staff spot, glad to see Bolin's hoity-toity SUV already there. By the time I'd been able to call him, he'd long since finished getting stitches in the ER and returned home. He'd been groggy on the phone and said he would talk to me in the morning, after acquiring coffee.

My wounds twinged as I eased out of the truck, and I wished I could rub pain-relief cream all over myself and sleep for a week. That wouldn't happen, but maybe I would get lucky and nobody would fill out a maintenance request today or come to complain about a noisy neighbor.

"Doubtful," I muttered.

Bolin stood in front of the office door with his two cups of coffee in hand, a black eye, and stitches above his eyebrow. I winced in sympathy. We *both* needed pain-relief cream.

"Sorry about the case," he said. "I shouldn't have brought it into this neighborhood at night."

Somehow, I doubted the *neighborhood* had been the problem. Crime might have been increasing a bit of late, but I still believed it had been a werewolf who'd attacked him.

"I shouldn't have *asked* you to bring it. It was safer where it was."

"Yeah."

"I'm sorry you got clobbered."

"Me too."

Surprisingly, Bolin offered me one of the coffees, the one in a simple paper cup with a flat lid. The iced whatever topped with whipped cream he clutched possessively to his chest.

"I thought you always got two for yourself," I said.

"I do, but you look even rougher than I do this morning."

I considered his tousled hair, stitches, black eye, and the slump to his shoulders.

"That's concerning."

"Yup. Did you sleep in the woods?" His gaze drifted toward a spot above my eyebrows.

My ponytail had long since fallen free, and my hair hung in tangles around my shoulders. I swept my hand back from my forehead, dislodging a few fir needles and a scale from a pine cone. The movement made my shoulder twinge, and I remembered my fall from the bridge. I'd been lucky not to break every bone in my body—or be shot. Fortunately, the bite wounds in my leg and hip weren't that bad. The locket had to have helped, at least in some minor way.

"I didn't sleep at all actually," I said.

"But the woods were involved, right?"

"The depths of the forest."

"A logical place to go in the middle of the night."

"For some." I accepted his coffee offering, taking a deep swig in case I needed to be alert that morning. A surprising hit of sweetness bathed my tongue. It was a mocha, the kind of thing I'd consumed in my twenties but that would now send my blood sugar levels on a roller coaster. Oh well. At least it seemed to have some extra shots of espresso in it.

"Being an intern here might not be as bad as I thought."

"Given how your night went, I'm surprised to hear that. What changed your mind?"

"You're weirder than I am."

"That's a plus?"

"You hardly ever stare at me like I'm a freak."

No, a kid with druid blood wasn't that strange when compared to someone who turned into a wolf and howled at the full moon.

"I've met some quirky people in my life," was all I said, wondering how long it would take him to figure out that I was one of them.

"Oh, there goes Mr. Davis." Bolin pointed toward the man with the plumbing and mold problem we'd been addressing. Bolin must have texted him, asking for permission to enter today, because a response popped up on his phone. After reading it, he said, "I can show you his apartment. It's all done."

"Okay." The last couple of days, I'd been so distracted that I'd half-forgotten about that issue. I did know the plumber had repaired the pipes and we'd had fans on in there to dry out the interior before putting the drywall back up.

"His apartment looks and smells so good now that you could

raise the rent." Bolin led me down the walkway toward the next building.

"As long as it's not moldy, and pipes aren't leaking, I'll be delighted."

"You'll be *more* than delighted." He walked faster, his back straight.

Was he proud? The kid who'd oozed resentment and superiority when he'd arrived and had made it clear he didn't want to be here?

When he unlocked the door and pushed it open, no hint of must wafted out of the apartment. Instead, the air smelled clean and faintly forest-like. I assumed the tenant had plugged an air freshener into an outlet, but when we walked inside, my senses pinged, picking up a faint hint of magic. A fern in a pot that hadn't been there before seemed to be the source.

"I trust you put that there, not the tenant." I pointed at it.

Bolin blinked in surprise. "How did you know?"

"It's oozing druidness."

"I enhanced it to clean the air even more than it naturally would. Of course, that isn't necessary because of the enchantment I found for in here." With a flourish of his arm, Bolin led me into the bathroom.

The repair work was done, fresh drywall and paint in place over the fixed pipes. The air also smelled clean in there, and I detected another slight hint of magic. It came from the walls—the paint?

"I applied the anti-mold paint you mentioned you kept in the maintenance shed, and I used it for a medium for my enchantment. It's extra *extra* anti-fungi now."

"All fungi? Not just mold?"

"Yeah, that's what the enchantment was for. I assumed we wouldn't want toadstools sprouting up in people's apartments either."

"No, and nobody needs to start a 'shroom grow lab in their bathroom either."

Bolin blinked. "Has that... happened?"

"Six times in the years I've worked here. It's *usually* marijuana, but one couple was doing mushrooms. I saw the delivery of wood chips and inoculation logs, or whatever they're called, and caught them."

"Huh."

"All right, thanks for taking care of all this." I clapped Bolin on the shoulder as we headed out.

"You'll tell my parents that I'm doing good work? Without, uhm... If you don't mention the druid oozing, that would be ideal. Especially if my mom is around."

"I wouldn't dream of mentioning it to anyone."

"Really?" Bolin squinted at me, as if he couldn't believe someone would keep his secrets for him.

"Really."

"Good. Thanks."

As I headed for my apartment to comb the rest of the forest out of my hair, shower, and put on fresh clothes, I decided having an intern might not be bad after all. Oh, I didn't expect Bolin would stay long—his parents would eventually give him the dream job they'd promised him—but maybe I could get him to mold-proof the rest of the units before he left.

When I unlocked my door and stepped into my living room, I sensed right away that someone had been there while I'd been gone. *He'd* been there. Duncan's scent lingered in the air.

I scowled at the door lock, as if it had betrayed me. The windows were securely closed, and I knew I hadn't left the door open. How had he gotten in?

"Bastard probably has a *magnet* that turns locks."

I stalked around the apartment, searching for anything that had been disturbed, though it wasn't as if there was much in there worth stealing. Just the wolf case. And he or someone else had already *gotten* that.

A small gift bag and an envelope on the table caught my eye. I squinted suspiciously at them. Duncan hadn't left me some hokey tchotchke in the hope that I would forgive him, had he? As if I could forgive him for working for Chad.

"Bastard," I grumbled again and strode toward the table.

I intended to tear up the envelope and hurl the gift bag in the trash without looking inside, but it clinked when I picked it up. That made me pause. Had he actually gotten my potions?

I pushed aside colorful tissue paper to draw out the contents. Four vials of liquid were nestled inside along with a business card. The name of the alchemist who'd made them? It said *apothecary*, but I knew witches rarely put their *real* business in print for people to find. This country didn't have a history of being kind toward those suspected of witchcraft.

At the bottom of the bag, there were also two dark-chocolate bars and a rusty fork. The fork he'd found in Lake Washington with me? Or another? I didn't know, but I flattened my hands on the table and stared at the gift, tears threatening my eyes. It wasn't so much that I was touched but that I was frustrated that he was the enemy instead of someone... someone I could let myself like.

"Bastard," I whispered for a third time, but I opened the envelope instead of tearing it up.

A card showed a cartoon dog in a fishing boat on a lake, holding out a rainbow trout in offering. It read *I'm sorry.*

Inside, Duncan had written a note in execrable handwriting that I struggled to decipher.

My apologies, my lady, for not being honest with you. When I accepted this mission—and, of course, the promise of adventure!—I didn't expect the wife that your loathed ex-husband had described to me would turn out to be an appealing person I'd like to know better. You may not believe it, but I enjoyed our time together. I've not had another wolf to hunt with in a long while. I hope you will accept this small gift as an adequate apology.

Best wishes,

Duncan

He hadn't left a phone number or any way to get in touch. It was for the best. I would accept his gift, but I still couldn't trust him. Nothing had changed. And it was entirely possible that he'd sent the thug who'd beaten up Bolin for the case.

Sighing, I walked into the bathroom with the vials. I studied them for a long moment, then removed the cork from one and sniffed the contents. The liquid looked and smelled correct. As promised, Duncan had found another alchemist who could make my potions, one who hadn't been scared off by a well-meaning but meddling relative.

Did I want to take the potion? A few days ago, I would have answered that question with a vehement *yes* and quaffed a dose. But things had changed, and I waffled with indecision.

On the one hand, dealing with cousins trying to kill me didn't make me eager to return to the embrace of my family—and the werewolf life. Nor did I feel good about the way the face-off with those hunters had gone, that I hadn't been able to control my rage, my animal instincts. Nothing, it seemed, had changed with time.

But, on the other hand, damn if I hadn't enjoyed being out there on the hunt. Even a hunt that had ended in disaster. Over the years, I'd forgotten the exhilaration, what it was like to truly be alive. It would be hard to give that up for a second time.

And my mother... My mother was dying, and she needed me. To turn my back on her, on our legacy, would be much harder to do today.

I thought of Mom's indifference to the deaths of the hunters, a similar indifference that she'd displayed years ago after Raoul's passing. I had been challenged by others, and I'd killed. That was just how it was. It was the way of the wolf.

It was as hard for me to accept that today as it had been then, but my gut told me that the future would bring more surprises, and it would be better to have power than not. All week, I hadn't heeded my gut when it had repeatedly warned me of danger, both with Duncan and with Augustus, and I'd regretted it.

"You win, Mom," I murmured.

I put the cork back in the vial and placed the potions in the medicine cabinet. For now, I would once again heed the call of the wolf.

THE END

Thank you for picking up Luna's story! I hope you enjoyed the adventure. If you have time to leave a review, I would appreciate it. If you'd like to read more, the adventure continues in Book 2, *Relics of the Wolf*.

For updates on new releases, sales, and the occasional bonus scene and free short story, please sign up for my fantasy newsletter:

https://lindsayburoker.com/book-news/